'How old are you?' Max demanded, ignoring her angry comment.

'If you must know, I'm twenty-four. Why?'

'At your age you should either be enjoying the present or looking forward to the future. Why aren't you?'

Fiona was so furious she jumped to her feet and stood in the middle of the pale honey-coloured carpet, glaring down at him. 'My future is my own affair, and I wish I could say the same of my present. Unfortunately you're also involved with that to a certain extent, but it doesn't give you the right to question me and invade my privacy.'

Max leaned back against the soft cream leather and looked up at her with half-closed eyes. 'Come down off your high horse and let me take you out to dinner,' he suggested lazily.

'Out to dinner?' she gasped. 'I—I wouldn't go out to dinner with you if—if you were the last man on earth!'

He laughed outright. 'Can't you think of anything more original than that?'

Clare Lavenham was born and brought up in London, but she has spent most of her life in Suffolk. She has a son and a daughter who was a nurse at the London Hospital. She has written articles, short stories and one-act plays, but it was because of her work as a hospital librarian that she turned to writing Medical Romances. She gets her backgrounds from her library work and consults various medical friends when necessary. Her favourite occupations, apart from writing, are walking in the country and gardening.

Previous Titles

WEB OF MEMORIES

BY

CLARE LAVENHAM

W.M.

V. Lucas   P.g.

MILLS & BOON LIMITED
ETON HOUSE   18–24 PARADISE ROAD
RICHMOND   SURREY   TW9 1SR

*First published in Great Britain 1990
by Mills & Boon Limited*

© Clare Lavenham 1990

*Australian copyright 1990
Philippine copyright 1990
This edition 1990*

ISBN 0 263 76982 8

*Set in 10 on 12 pt Linotron Times
03-9009-49038
Typeset in Great Britain by Centracet, Cambridge
Made and printed in Great Britain*

CHAPTER ONE

FIONA had started to look out for the signpost much too early. She was beginning to doubt her map-reading when the headlights picked out its pointing arm. 'Tarling 2 miles.'

She was tired after the eighty-mile run from London, for the traffic on the A12 had been heavy, but in the midst of her relief at being so near her journey's end, a tiny prickle of excitement caused her heart to beat a little faster. The emotion was short-lived. As she swung her Metro off the main road into a much narrower one with overhanging trees, the doubts which had tormented her at intervals all the way returned with renewed force.

Would this tremendous upheaval in her life turn out to be as beneficial as she hoped? Or was it the daftest thing she had ever done?

The tangle of minor roads in which she now found herself caused her once more to shelve her problem and concentrate on not taking a wrong turning. The signposts were inclined to be unhelpful, but eventually she came to one which informed her that she was only half a mile from her destination.

It was then that she noticed the blue flashing lights somewhere ahead. Easing her foot off the accelerator, Fiona stared at them in dismay. She definitely didn't want to get involved in an accident, and so near the village too.

It was impossible to get any idea of what was going on because a sharp bend with high hedges blocked her view. Driving more and more slowly, she approached it with caution. As she rounded the corner, she found her way blocked by the police car whose warning lights had alerted her. There was also another car with its headlights full on and a sickening mass of torn metal which had once been two more cars, now locked in a deadly embrace.

Fiona hated accidents. Her mouth was dry and her hands shook as she turned the Metro on to the grass verge. Getting out, she reminded herself sternly that she was a nurse. Very few people knew about her secret shame, and she had even managed to conceal it through six years of working at a busy London hospital, including a spell in the accident unit which ought to have cured her but had failed dismally.

'Afraid you can't get through this way, miss.' A tall young policeman had loomed up beside her. 'You'll have to turn your car and take a different route. Where are you heading for?'

'Tarling.' Fiona was relieved to find her voice gave no clue to her feelings. 'It's quite near, isn't it?'

'It would be if you could still keep on this road. As it is, you'll have to return to the last crossroads and then——'

'I can't do that,' she interrupted him, 'at least, not yet. I'm a nurse, you see, and I wondered if I could help.'

His whole manner changed instantly and became briskly efficient. 'I reckon the doctor could do with another pair of hands. There's folks in the Volvo urgently needing attention.'

Much relieved to find that a doctor was on the scene, Fiona followed the police officer down the road towards the two cars which had apparently collided head-on with such force that the Mini was now buried in the bonnet of the larger vehicle.

'Here's a young lady offering to help, Doctor.'

'What?' The man standing with his head inside the Volvo on the driver's side withdrew briefly, revealing an unruly thatch of tawny hair and a pair of angry eyes above a strong nose and a square chin with a cleft in it. 'There's nothing here for well-meaning amateurs, Officer. Tell her to get the hell out of it.'

The arrogance of the man! He was obviously one of those doctors who thought themselves God's gift to mankind, and everybody else very much lesser fry. Fiona had met them in hospital now and then, and heartily disliked the breed.

Before the policeman could reply, she took a step forward and said, coolly, 'I happen to be a nurse, but if there's nothing I can do I shall be only too glad to resume my journey as quickly as possible.'

'A nurse, eh?' His tone had changed, but not very much. 'There's not a lot anyone can do, because the doors are jammed, but I suppose you could try to calm the passenger.'

'Certainly.' She glanced over her shoulder at the Mini. 'Is he——?'

'Alive? Just about. I managed to check that his airway is clear, but nothing else can be done until cutting gear arrives.' He flung her an impatient look. 'I'd be obliged if you would do as I asked, before she has hysterics. I've got my hands full with this chap.'

Fiona hurried round the back of the car and found a

shattered window. Cautiously she put her head in and discovered a girl with blood running down her face, still held by her seatbelt. She was alternately screaming and sobbing, and seemed almost out of her mind with terror. As always when there was something to be done, Fiona's squeamishness left her, and she captured one of the bloodstained hands and held it firmly, talking meanwhile in her most soothing voice.

Eventually she got her patient sufficiently calmed down to learn that her terror was not for herself but for her husband. Glancing across, Fiona saw the doctor administering an injection and guessed it was a pain-killer. The man clearly had chest injuries and was only semi-conscious, but it would be difficult to tell how badly he was hurt until he reached hospital. There did not seem to be much wrong with his wife.

'Why don't they get us out?' The girl's voice threatened to rise again. 'Nobody seems to be doing a thing about it——'

'It's because the doors won't open.' Fiona found a clean handkerchief in her pocket and wiped away some of the blood. At that moment her ear caught the sound of sirens in the distance. 'I think help is on the way, so try to be brave for a little longer, love.'

The ambulance and the rescue vehicle arrived one behind the other, and the scene became one of ordered confusion. Standing back out of the way, Fiona watched as the two prisoners were released and then resumed her attendance on the girl, while her husband was carefully transferred to a stretcher by two cheerful and efficient ambulancemen, closely watched by the doctor.

Now that she had time to look at him, she realised

he was wearing a sort of yellow tabard with the word 'DOCTOR' across the back of it. It was a good idea, she was obliged to admit, but she didn't think there could be many medical men who kept one in the car in case of need.

As the ambulance sped off, she glanced at the Mini, where the firemen were already busy with their cutting gear. And suddenly all her hatred of accidents returned and she felt sick. There was a mangled human being in there and she couldn't bear to think of the state he must be in. But she could hardly disappear without a word to the doctor after offering her services, so she went across to where he stood watching with his hands on his hips.

'Damn silly young fool!' he growled. 'There's never any excuse for head-on collisions.'

Fiona let that pass. 'Do you think there's any hope at all?'

'How the devil should I know? I'm not clairvoyant.' He scowled at her.

'I didn't imagine you were,' she said icily.

He gave her a sharp look from beneath strongly marked brows that matched his hair. To her surprise she thought she noticed a gleam of amusement in the startlingly blue eyes, but it vanished so quickly she felt sure she must be mistaken. There was certainly no amusement in his voice when he answered her.

'Silly questions deserve silly answers. You might bear that in mind, Nurse.'

On the verge of an angry reply, Fiona reined in her temper. She wasn't likely to meet him again and there was no point in quarrelling with him. 'Thank you so much, Doctor,' she said sweetly. 'I shall certainly take your advice to heart.'

Fortunately the policeman chose that moment to appear on her other side. 'This road won't be open for some time, so there's no point in your waiting. Much better drive back to the crossroads as I said and take the other route. That is,' he said hastily, 'if Dr Whitmore doesn't need you any more.'

'He never did need me,' she said swiftly, before the doctor could beat her to it. 'Which road do I take when I get to the crossroads?'

He gave her careful directions and, after turning her car with some difficulty, she drove off. Behind her, Max Whitmore watched the tail-lights disappear round the bend and experienced a brief moment of regret. She'd meant well, he supposed, and he was afraid he had been abominably rude. If only he had not been so bloody tired after being up most of the night, he might have controlled his irritation better.

Or, on the other hand, he might not. He had sensed her reluctance and he guessed she had offered to help from nothing warmer than a sense of duty. No doubt the accident—which was more than likely to result in a young man losing his life—had been no more to her than a tiresome interruption to her journey.

He hadn't much use for people like that.

With a mental shrug, he dismissed the nurse from his mind and gave his full attention to the progress being made by the men with their powerful equipment. They seemed to be getting on well and it was now much easier for him to reach into the crushed car and try to find a pulse. It was still beating but, nevertheless, he did not rate the chances of the injured man very high.

And if this one turned out to be DOA, he would be the third certified dead on arrival at hospital in the last month. It was enough to make anyone feel angry and depressed.

Fiona was also having a moment of regret. She ought not to have let Dr Whitmore get under her skin like that. If she'd tried to radiate calmness and efficiency instead of being abrasive, they might have got on better.

Watching the beam of her headlights on an empty road was having a calming effect, and by the time she reached the outskirts of Tarling she had dismissed the accident entirely from her mind. In any case, she now had other thoughts to engage her attention, memories of a ten-year-old girl who had believed the village to be very close to paradise, and who had looked forward to her annual holiday there with a longing which was never disappointed.

Would it have changed very much? Trying to be sensible, she had convinced herself that change was inevitable, and it was wonderful to find the main street looking just as she remembered it, except for the addition of an elegantly painted village sign.

There was the miniature green, with its spreading chestnut tree still standing in spite of the hurricane a couple of years ago. The stumpy tower of the church had scaffolding round it, but that, she hoped, would only be temporary, and the bridge over the infant River Tarl was still only one vehicle wide, no doubt causing even more trouble than in the past.

Fiona halted her car outside a prosperous-looking antique shop and drew a great breath of relief. In her secret heart she hadn't been a bit sure about this return to the past. Nostalgia was like a drug—it would be easy to let it get too strong a hold. Wasn't it generally considered better to concentrate on the future and let bygones slumber beneath their dust undisturbed?

The trouble was she had no future. It had vanished one cold January morning, leaving her nothing but memories which were so painful she could not contemplate them without tears. Surely it was far better to dredge up those other, more distant memories and reply to the advertisement for a job in Tarling, seen by chance in the *Nursing Times*? In Tarling she had been happy. Perhaps she could learn to become so again.

Finding the village looking much the same seemed like a good omen. Optimistically, Fiona restarted the engine and drove on. People tended to go to bed early in the country and Miss Crane, with whom she was to stay, was probably waiting up for her and getting worried. She could not recall a house called Apple Acre, but the address—Glebe Lane—suggested it was near the church, and she soon found the dark turning by the side of the graveyard. There was a row of cottages on the right and then a gap, after which an attractive pink-washed cottage stood alone.

Fiona was groping for a torch when the front door opened and a stream of amber light poured out into the small front garden. A cream Labrador burst out, barking furiously but with wagging tail, and behind the dog a small, grey-haired figure in cord trousers called out eagerly, 'Is that you, Nurse Shelton?'

Acknowledging her identity with a smile and an apology for being so late, Fiona, a tall girl, looked down at her petite landlady with interest. Miss Crane, she guessed, was in her early fifties and she looked a picture of health with her fresh colour and bright eyes. Her skin was hardly lined at all and, far from longing for her bed, she exuded boundless energy.

'Come right in, dear,' she invited, holding the door wide and pushing the Labrador out of the way. 'You must be tired after that long drive, so we'll let your luggage stay where it is for the moment and concentrate on a reviving drink. Which shall it be, whisky or Horlicks?'

Fiona did not much care for either, but she felt the need of something and chose a well watered down whisky, which was served with a plate of cheese-flavoured biscuits. Sipping cautiously, she glanced round the room with appreciation. It was shabby, chintzy and comfortable, with exposed beams and a real fire.

'It gets chilly in the evenings even though it's nearly the end of April.' Miss Crane threw on another log. 'Did you have a good journey?'

'There was a lot of traffic most of the way.' Fiona hesitated and felt an irresistible urge to talk about the accident. 'The traffic didn't bother me too much and I'd have been here much sooner if it hadn't been for what happened when I was only half a mile away.' She gave a brief account of her adventure, making it merely factual, or so she thought.

'I think the two in the Volvo will probably be all right,' she finished, 'but I don't know about the Mini driver.'

'Poor chap. It may have been all his fault, but one can't help feeling sorry for him. I expect he was young.

Did Max Whitmore stay with him until he was released?'

'I imagine so.' Fiona stared at the small, alert figure on the other side of the hearth. 'How did you know that was his name?'

'You said the doctor had arrived well in advance of the ambulance and I guessed it must be Max.'

'Do you know him, then?'

Miss Crane burst out laughing. 'Of course I do! Didn't it occur to you that he might be a member of the practice you're going to join?'

'N-no—I just thought he happened to be passing through.'

The news was a shock, and Fiona felt shattered as she viewed the prospect of working with a man to whom she had taken such an intense dislike. She had liked old Dr McBride, the senior partner, who had interviewed her in London and offered her the job, and she had not worried much about the other three members of the practice, assuming they would be a mixed bunch and leaving it at that.

'Somehow I get the impression you didn't exactly take to Dr Whitmore. Am I right?'

'Horribly right!' Fiona tried to speak lightly. 'To be honest, I thought he was one of the rudest doctors I've ever met, and I've come across a few in my time.'

'Oh, dear, poor Max must have been in a black mood, or else desperately tired. He works much too hard and I often think the others take advantage of his being the youngest and newest partner. Except for Maggie McBride, of course, and she's the old man's daughter and in a privileged position.'

Fiona reached out her hand and took another of the

delicious biscuits—homemade, she guessed. 'I thought the work was more or less evenly divided out in a group practice.'

'Theoretically, yes, but it doesn't always work out that way. But the real reason for Max getting overworked is this County Accident Rescue Service he belongs to. As you know, we're not very far from the A12, and there are a lot of accidents in this area.'

Fiona had never heard of the Service. It sounded a good idea, and she was about to ask for further details when she was overtaken by an immense yawn. The warmth of the fire and the unaccustomed whisky on top of a long and tiring journey were having the inevitable effect.

Her hostess glanced at her and smiled. 'It's high time I showed you your room. Would you like another drink first?'

'No, thank you, Miss Crane.'

'For goodness' sake don't call me that, Fiona! My name is Elizabeth, but everybody calls me Liz, including my patients.'

'Patients?'

'I'm a reflexologist, dear, and if that means nothing to you I won't bother you with an explanation now.' She stood up and collected the two empty glasses. 'As for your new job, if there's anything you want to know before you start work, you can ask me at breakfast. I'm a mine of information on both doctors and patients— and so I should be, considering that until a year or so ago *I* was the nurse attached to the practice.'

'I thought you said you were—something else,' Fiona exclaimed.

'Reflexologist, but that's a recent development. I

trained at the local hospital, worked there for some years and then became Dr McBride's nurse when he had only one partner. I watched the practice grow over the years and there's nothing I don't know about it. I'm at your service!'

'Great!' Fiona stifled another yawn. 'I'll fetch my luggage from the car, but I don't think I'll do much unpacking tonight.' Following Liz to the front door, she continued apologetically, 'I'm afraid I've got an awful lot, but you do rather tend to collect things when you're nursing at the same hospital for six years.'

'It doesn't matter to me, dear, but wasn't there anywhere you could leave some of it?'

There was a short pause and then Fiona said curtly, 'Afraid not.'

Liz made no comment. Between them they soon carried in three suitcases, two holdalls and a large plastic bag. The stairs were easy, with a half-landing and only ten steps altogether, although there were a few more odd ones on the first floor. Fiona was delighted to be shown to a large room at the back which had been furnished as a bedsitting-room with a desk and comfortable chair as well as built-in cupboards and a Vanitory unit.

Having unpacked the barest minimum, she undressed and got into bed. Within a few minutes she was asleep.

She was awake early, pleased to find that the weariness, uncertainty and slight depression she had experienced the evening before had all vanished. It was a sparkling morning and she gazed out at it in delight. Down below there was a patio, a lawn with flowerbeds, and then the apple orchard which gave the house its name. The trees were in bud and would present a wonderful picture when they were out.

Fiona would have liked to pull on the jeans and sweater she had worn yesterday and set out to explore, but the sight of her uniform dress laid out over the back of a chair reminded her that she must be at the surgery by eight-thirty.

When she was dressed, she paused for a moment in front of the mirror and looked at herself critically, determined that even the unpleasant Dr Whitmore should find no fault with her appearance. She was lucky that the dark blue dress looked good with her pale gold hair, worn loose yesterday but now folded into a neat pleat at the back of her head. If she had had blue eyes the effect might have been even better, but hers were a dark velvety brown and provided a wonderful contrast to her hair.

Satisfied, she turned away from the mirror, quite unaware that the secret unhappiness she believed to be safely hidden in her heart showed quite plainly—to a discerning viewer—in the depths of her eyes and the straightness of lips which had been fashioned for laughter and kisses.

'You know where the surgery is, I suppose?' Liz asked as Fiona put on her raincoat and picked up her bag.

'Dr McBride said it was a new building in East Lane.'

'That's right. It's on the left.'

Fiona intended to walk most mornings, but she decided to take her car this first morning, just in case she needed it for something. She drove past the antique shops, a surprisingly elegant dress shop and a small supermarket. Turning into East Lane, she immediately noticed the new brick building standing a little back from the roadway. There was one car parked outside and a bicycle propped up in the cycle rack.

Inside, she found a sort of foyer with rows of chairs and a number of doors opening all round. Facing her was the reception counter, where a girl with a great deal of curly brown hair, and wearing a white coat, stood talking to a man with his back turned.

If she had not been alerted by her hostess, Fiona would not have recognised that broad back so easily. As it was, her heart sank. She had so hoped Max Whitmore would not be the first doctor she would meet.

Determined to make the best of it, she said brightly to the receptionist, 'Hello! I'm Fiona Shelton.'

'The new nurse?' The small face half hidden by riotous curls broke into a friendly smile. 'I'm Anne Marshall, and this is Dr Whitmore.'

Fiona held her breath as he turned round. She must look very different in her uniform from the girl who had loomed out of the darkness last night. It would be a lucky break if he didn't recognise her.

There was no recognition in the vivid blue eyes, which looked her up and down critically. He said, 'Good morning,' rather curtly, and it seemed to her that the accompanying smile was mechanical rather than friendly. Instinctively she tilted her head a little higher and pretended not to notice his scrutiny, though she did reply to his greeting in a cool, courteous voice.

'I expect Dr McBride explained to you what your duties would be?' he enquired.

'Yes, thank you, Doctor,' Fiona said demurely.

'I believe you're a stranger to this area,' he ploughed

on. 'Have you been able to find somewhere to live which is reasonably near?'

'Oh, yes—it's no distance at all. I'm going to stay with Miss Crane at Apple Acre.' Confident that he would approve, she glanced up at him with a half-smile.

But to her amazement the information was received with a look of thunder. '*That* woman!' he exclaimed incredulously.

CHAPTER TWO

FIONA had set out that morning with the laudable intention of giving Dr Whitmore a second chance. After all, if they were going to work together it was clearly better that they should get on. But his reaction to her innocent mention of Miss Crane had flung their relationship back to square one.

Anne Marshall gave her a rueful look, raised her eyebrows slightly and went off to answer the phone. As Fiona struggled to think of a suitable reply, the doctor appeared to get a grip on his temper.

He said more calmly, 'Your room is at the back, Nurse, next to the dispensary. I hope you'll find everything you need, but if you run into any difficulty, I'm sure Anne can help you.'

It was clearly impossible to challenge him about that devastating comment just now. Transferring it to the back of her mind but giving it priority over the other items stored there—such as the meaning of reflexologist—Fiona went off to familiarise herself with the surgery complex.

It was single-storey and had been custom-built in Dr McBride's large garden. His house—Victorian in style—stood next to it, but there was no sign of the man himself, and Anne told her it was his day off.

'Dr Maggie will be in soon, I expect,' she said, her busy hands searching through a box of patients' cards as she spoke. 'She's usually early, but she got called out to an emergency.'

Fiona was wondering why they didn't store their records on disks, but all she said was, 'What about the other doctor?'

'Dr Kennedy hasn't got a clinic today. We never have more than two doctors on duty here at any one time because there's another surgery at Bedgrave.'

The name had rung a bell, and Fiona groped for an elusive memory. Wasn't Bedgrave the place where her grandparents had used to take her to pick plums?

While they were talking another receptionist, an older woman, had arrived and also the dispenser, and the waiting-room was nearly half full. As Fiona turned towards her own domain, the outer door opened and a girl not much older than herself came in with a rush. She was rather oddly dressed in maroon trousers and a scarlet sweater—not a happy choice of colours—and had a round face which was fresh-coloured and homely looking. Her smile was bright and friendly.

'Hi!' She held out a hand and shook Fiona's vigorously. 'You must be Nurse Shelton. I'm Maggie McBride.'

Not waiting for a reply, she went hurrying off to her consulting-room and almost immediately summoned a patient. Glad that she had met a doctor whom she instinctively liked, Fiona began to prepare for a mother and baby clinic which the nurse's timetable informed her was due at ten o'clock. After being a senior staff nurse on a surgical ward, she found the work was unfamiliar, and she hoped the mothers wouldn't notice her slight nervousness.

When everything was ready, she went out to the

reception area to see if they had all arrived. Nine pairs of eyes from an assortment of youngish women immediately fastened on her with frank curiosity, but before she could summon the first tiny patient and attendant mum, a middle-aged woman suddenly stood up and confronted her.

'Excuse me, Nurse. . .'

'Yes?' Fiona paused, anxious to begin her clinic but nevertheless giving the woman her full attention. 'Can I help you?'

'It's nothing medical and perhaps I shouldn't have bothered you just now, but I didn't know if I'd get another chance. It's your name, you see. I heard Dr Maggie call you Nurse Shelton and I wondered if you were any relation of some people of that name who used to live here.'

Fiona's eyes lit up with interest. 'At a house called Cornerways?'

'That's right. My husband, George Walsh, was their gardener. They were a lovely couple, it was a dreadful tragedy they both died in that awful accident.'

'I was in it too, but thrown clear.' A shadow crossed Fiona's face, but she did not mention the horror that still lingered. 'They were my grandparents, and I often stayed with them when I was a child.'

Mrs Walsh's lined face broke into a smile. 'They say it's a small world, don't they? Whoever would have thought you'd turn up in Tarling?'

'It wasn't actually chance. I happened to see an advert——'

Fiona broke off abruptly as she suddenly became aware that Max Whitmore had emerged from his room and was watching them. He made an impatient gesture, as though inviting her into his sanctum.

'One moment, Nurse.'

She did not move. 'I have a clinic just now,' she said coolly. 'Can't it wait?'

His thick, tufty eyebrows shot up. 'So you *did* know about the clinic? I wondered whether you were aware of it.'

'Perfectly aware, thank you. Was that all you wanted?'

Her voice was quiet and controlled, but inside she was boiling. She would have liked to hit him, but, although it would have relieved her feelings, it would scarcely have improved their relationship, or her standing with the patients.

Mrs Walsh had sat down again in some embarrassment. Fiona deliberately turned her back on the doctor and gave her a friendly smile.

'I'm very grateful to you for speaking to me. We must meet again some time, *away* from the surgery, and have a lovely long talk.'

Her head held high, she marched back to her room and began the clinic, which had been delayed by no more than a minute. Surprisingly, she found her nervousness had entirely vanished. But whether it had been banished by a meeting with someone from the beloved past, or the anger aroused by her brief conversation with the doctor, Fiona was not prepared to say.

By the time she had finished, the waiting patients had all gone and both doctors had started their rounds. She spent the rest of the morning in a further exploration of cupboards and drawers so that she could quickly find anything which was required.

'What are you doing for lunch?' Anne appeared suddenly in the doorway. 'I usually go to the Fox and have a snack. Like to join me?'

Fiona accepted with alacrity and the two girls walked down East Lane to the High Street. As they went, Anne explained that her husband was a schoolteacher and had his lunch at school, so, although they lived in the village, she rarely went home in the middle of the day.

'You're married!' Fiona exclaimed, and added frankly, 'Somehow you don't look it.'

Anne burst out laughing. 'What's that supposed to mean?'

'Nothing—forget it.'

'I expect you think I look young and irresponsible. Most people do. Actually, I'm nineteen and Simon is twenty-two. How old are you?'

'Twenty-four,' said Fiona, feeling like a spinster aunt.

Anne made no comment. 'I would have been quite willing for us to live together for a trial period,' she confided, 'but Simon's old-fashioned. It was marriage or nothing for him—would you believe it? I didn't want to lose him, so I agreed, but sometimes. . .' She sighed and left the sentence unfinished.

They reached the Fox, a pretty place with window-boxes full of tulips, and went inside. When they were settled in a corner with Coke and sandwiches, Anne resumed the conversation.

'I hope you don't mind my asking. Have you got a steady relationship with anybody?'

The question caught Fiona unprepared and her first instinct was to say, 'No,' and leave it at that. It was, after all, the truth. But she liked Anne and sensed that her curiosity was based on an interest in people rather than mere nosiness.

'There's no man in my life,' she said tautly, 'and that's the way I want to keep it. For a long time, anyway. Three months ago I was going to marry a doctor at the same hospital, but he ditched me almost at the last moment because he found someone he liked better. It was a humiliating experience which I have no intention of allowing to happen again.'

It had taken her three months to make herself believe that the humiliation had been the worst part, but at the time she had been utterly shattered, her heart torn, bruised and bleeding. Somehow she had hidden her unhappiness from her friends and kept her end up, but the effort had taken its toll. Consequently, she had made the difficult decision to uproot herself and look round for a less exacting job which would also be a complete change.

'That was rotten for you.' Anne was silent for a moment, chewing thoughtfully, then she asked, 'What made you come to a funny little backwater like Tarling?'

'Nostalgia. I have happy memories of holidays here when I was a kid.'

Feeling that she had revealed quite enough of herself for one day, Fiona decided to change the subject. This was a good opportunity to find out a bit more about the unpleasant Dr Whitmore—so long as talking about him didn't give her indigestion! Consequently she asked Anne if she could explain why he had exclaimed, 'That woman!' when she'd mentioned Liz Crane.

'It's because she's a reflexologist.'

That word again! It seemed that the two questions Fiona most wanted to find an answer for were turning into one.

'Liz mentioned last night that she was one of those,' she said, 'but we were just going to bed and we shelved an explanation until this morning, but somehow there wasn't time at breakfast because we were busy talking about the practice. What *is* a reflexologist? I don't think I've ever heard of it.'

'It's a form of what they call alternative medicine. You know—like osteopathy and chiropractice and acupuncture.'

'I've heard of all those, and I thought osteopaths at least were usually accepted by doctors these days.'

Anne looked vague. 'We don't have any in Tarling, but we *do* have Miss Crane calling herself a reflexologist. Max Whitmore doesn't approve of her at all, and that's why he was so angry. He thinks she's a dangerous woman.'

'And is she?'

'Shouldn't think so.' Anne smiled. 'She only tickles the soles of people's feet and, apart from making them die laughing, I can't see it's likely to do any harm.'

'Or any good either,' Fiona suggested lightly.

'She cured my mother-in-law when she had a painful shoulder.' Anne ate the last piece of sandwich and pushed the plate away. 'What did you think of our Dr Max?' she asked after a pause.

Fiona took a deep breath. 'He's a very—macho type,' she said cautiously.

'You can say that again! Personally I think he's rather gorgeous, and the patients absolutely adore him.' Seeing Fiona's look of astonishment, she added hastily, 'I meant, of course, the ones who are really ill. He can't stand the others and doesn't mind letting them see it.'

'I can imagine.' Fiona hesitated and then surprised herself by saying, 'I don't think he approves of me either. I get the feeling he's just waiting for me to make a bad mistake.'

'You could be right, but there's a reason for it. We've been terribly unlucky with our nurses ever since Liz Crane resigned. There were four of them, and one left to nurse her mother and another got pregnant, and the other two were bored with the job and not at all conscientious, and they got sacked.' Anne leaned her arms on the table and looked earnestly into Fiona's face. 'Dr McBride was over the moon when you—a top London staff nurse—applied for the job. Everybody's watching you to see if you'll settle down. Do you think you will?'

Fiona was feeling so much better now that Dr Whitmore's animosity was explained that she answered almost gaily, 'I certainly hope so,' and went on to tell the receptionist all about her childhood visits to the village.

Soon it was time to start work again. Two mothers were bringing their babies for inoculations that afternoon, and no sooner had they been dealt with than a farm worker arrived with a severely cut hand. Fiona cleaned him up and put on a sterile dressing, telling the man to return at evening surgery time to be properly stitched.

She was sitting in her room enjoying a much-needed cup of tea when the telephone rang.

It was Max Whitmore. At the sound of his crisp

tones Fiona felt herself tensing slightly. After her conversation with Anne she had decided to give him another chance—the third, wasn't it?—but she was very wary of him all the same.

'I want you to join me at the old people's flats at the top of the High Street, number seventeen. One of Dr McBride's patients doesn't approve of me as a substitute. Come at once, please, I've wasted enough time already.'

He rang off before she could say anything. Presumably he took it for granted he had only to summon the nurse and she would come running—or, more accurately, at the wheel of her car.

Fiona looked at the half-empty cup in front of her and finished the tea in a gulp. In less than two minutes she had reached the flats. The door of number seventeen stood wide open and she went straight in, to find Max pacing impatiently up and down the living-room.

He glowered at her. 'You took your time!'

'I most certainly did not! I finished a cup of tea, which took about two seconds, and then went straight out to my car and drove here as fast as practicable. What seems to be the trouble?'

He gave her a suspicious stare, but she kept her face carefully expressionless, and he went on to tell her about the case. 'This lady suffers from excessive modesty. I'm fairly sure she's got a strangulated inguinal hernia, but she won't let me examine her. I'm hoping you can persuade her.'

They were standing very close to each other as he talked in a low voice. Fiona could see the tiny golden hairs on his cheekbones and the incipient wrinkles at the corner of his eyes. Laughter lines? Surely not! They were far more likely to be caused by over-much frowning.

With an abrupt movement she broke free and went over to the bed on the far side of the room. The flat was really no more than a big bedsitting-room with a minute kitchen and bathroom opening out of it, but it was nicely furnished in an old-fashioned sort of way and very tidy. The patient was lying in a curled-up position, her white hair neatly plaited and her face grey with pain.

'Here's the nurse to see you, Miss Pennington,' the doctor called out.

Fiona took one of the blue-veined hands and held it. 'I hear you've been having some rather bad pain,' she said gently. 'Would you like to tell me about it?'

'Where's Dr McBride?' the woman asked querulously. 'He's my doctor and I want to see him.'

'I'm afraid it's his day off——'

'Day off? They never used to have days off. Always ready to come when you needed them, they were in the old days.'

'I know, but nothing's the same as it used to be, unfortunately.' Taking permission for granted, Fiona carefully pulled down the bedclothes and exposed a flannelette nightgown. She managed to draw it up sufficiently to uncover the painful area and, with a tactful arrangement of the sheet, contrived to leave no more of Miss Pennington's thin body on view than was necessary.

'It must have been hurting you quite a lot,' she said sympathetically, 'but the doctor thinks he knows what the trouble is. If I stay right here beside you, will you let him have a look? Just to make sure he's right.'

Miss Pennington did not reply, but she closed her eyes and clung to Fiona's hand. Cautiously, Max approached and made his examination.

'As I thought,' he said quietly when he had withdrawn and Fiona had rearranged the bedclothes. 'I shall have to request her immediate admission.'

'Which hospital will it be?'

'The big new general at Easterwood.'

Miss Pennington had caught the word 'hospital' and began a panic-stricken protest. Max hastily retreated towards the door.

'I'll go and make the necessary phone call,' he said hurriedly. 'I'm sure you'll be able to cope.'

Fiona surprised herself by mouthing 'coward' at him, but he did not appear to notice, and then she began the task of persuading the old lady to accept hospitalisation. It was accomplished with difficulty, and she departed to put the warden of the flats in the picture. The woman, who seemed kind and sympathetic, readily promised to pack a small case for Miss Pennington and see her off when the ambulance came.

Fiona was back in her own room at the surgery, and catching up on some paperwork, when Max suddenly appeared in the doorway.

'Everything OK?' he asked.

'No problem,' she assured him without looking up.

She could feel his eyes on her, but she continued to write with apparent concentration, though her hand trembled slightly. Why on earth was the wretched man having this effect on her? She still didn't like him, though she had revised her original opinion a little.

'Thanks for your help.' He flung the words at her as though they had been a missile and departed abruptly.

Fiona smiled to herself. One up to her, she reflected smugly, and continued with her work.

That evening Liz was eager to have an account of her day, and Fiona gave it to her in full, including a frank appraisal of the junior partner.

'I have to admit I find him very difficult to get on with,' she sighed. 'I can't think why everybody seems to speak so highly of him—except old Miss Pennington, and she was only prejudiced because of his youth.'

'He's a very good docor and nothing is too much trouble for him. He's compassionate too, or he wouldn't have lumbered himself with the Accident Rescue Service. It's all voluntary work, you know.' Liz cut two generous slices of lemon meringue pie. 'You'll have to ignore his abrasive manner.'

Fiona thought about it before she replied. She had never been able to understand why people couldn't be reasonably polite to each other in the course of normal life. It made things so much easier.

'I'm quite willing to do my share towards an agreeable relationship,' she said at last, 'but I'm not going to do all the work. If I've got to get used to him, he'll have to accept me as I am too.'

Liz laughed. 'I'm not at all sure which of you to back, so I think I'll just wait on the sidelines to see who wins!'

Fiona ate her helping of lemon pie and accepted a second. When she was assisting to clear away, she said diffidently, 'I'm surprised you speak so highly of Max Whitmore. You must know he doesn't approve of—of your work.'

'Of course I know, but I try to be objective about it.' Liz turned on the hot tap and waited for the bowl to fill. 'People who practise alternative medicine are bound to run up against opposition from conventional practitioners. The really remarkable thing is that Dr McBride, who's so much older and set in his ways, is keeping an open mind on the subject of reflexology.'

'Perhaps it's because of his regard for you.'

Liz looked startled. 'Could be, I suppose, but I hope not. I'd much rather he took an objective view.'

'What about Dr Maggie and—what's the other one's name?'

'David Kennedy. I think Maggie is interested, but Dr Kennedy couldn't care less. Since his wife died, he hasn't taken much interest in anything, poor chap, but I suppose it's understandable.'

Fiona dried a glass with care and then said, 'You still haven't told me what reflexology is all about. Anne said you tickle the soles of people's feet, but I didn't really believe that.'

'It's much harder work than tickling, and some people complain that it hurts. What I do is to manipulate every part of the patient's feet with my hands, the theory being that all the nerves in the body end in the feet and by treating the nerve-ends you affect the whole person.'

'What sort of complaints does it cure?' Fiona was doing her best not to sound sceptical and finding it rather difficult.

'Practically anything, but mostly joint pain and strained muscles. My patients lie very comfortably on a sofa with their feet high on an outsize cushion, and I sit at the end and we have interesting conversations.' Liz tipped out the washing-up water and hung out the cloth. 'There are some things I would never attempt to cure, like cancer and various conditions which need an operation, but on the whole most people benefit considerably from their treatment.'

Going upstairs to tackle her neglected unpacking, Fiona thought about what she had been told. She liked Liz immensely and instinctively trusted her judgement. She surely wouldn't devote the remainder of her working life to what sounded like utter rubbish unless she was quite sure it was *not* rubbish?

It was all very puzzling, but if wise old Dr McBride was keeping an open mind there was no reason why his new nurse shouldn't attempt to do the same. She certainly had no intention of copying the ridiculous prejudice displayed by Max Whitmore!

Shying away from such an unpleasant subject, Fiona concentrated on finding somewhere for her numerous possessions, and by the end of the evening she had arranged everything to her satisfaction, so that she now felt thoroughly at home at Apple Acre.

It couldn't really be said that she felt equally at home in the practice, but she hoped that would come. In the morning it was a help when Dr McBride looked in to see her before driving over to the other surgery at Bedgrave, and she greeted him with pleasure.

He was a big man with a grizzled beard and keen grey eyes, and his handshake almost caused Fiona to wince with pain.

'How did you get on yesterday?' he asked.

'OK, I think,' she assured him cheerfully, ignoring her resentment of Dr Whitmore's attitude towards her.

'That's good.' He beamed at her. 'I hope you'll be happy here, my dear, and stay with us for some time.

We've had too many changes recently and the patients don't like it. Nor do the doctors.'

'I can understand that, Doctor,' Fiona said quietly. 'I certainly hope to stay.'

But in her own mind she was not quite as definite as she had sounded. It all depended on whether this return to her grass roots would turn out to be a good thing, and she wouldn't find that out until she had revisited her grandparents' house, so much loved in the past, and discovered what emotions it aroused in her.

CHAPTER THREE

SATURDAY was Max's day off and he was really looking forward to it. He suspected it was partly because he would have the house to himself since his sister, who had lived with him recently, intended to go away for the weekend. He was sorry for Rachel, who was separated from her husband, but he found the constant reiteration of her marital problems very hard to bear at the end of a long day.

He would be able, weather permitting, to spend the whole day in the garden, eat when he felt like it, get as dirty as he liked, and even bring some of his dirt into the house so long as he cleaned it up before Rachel got back. After a somewhat trying week, the prospect seemed very like paradise, though he knew he wouldn't want to live like that for long.

He had a luxurious lie-in and a large, late breakfast. By then the sun had come out and, clad in shorts and dark blue T-shirt, and carrying a spade, Max went down to the far end of the long garden and began to prepare a site for runner beans. He enjoyed gardening, not only because it helped him to unwind but because it made him feel closer to the country patients he treated every day. If he could ask a man whether he had got his main-crop potatoes in yet, or how his roses were doing, he could more easily make the patient feel sufficiently relaxed to talk about his deepest worries.

Rachel thought it was a load of rubbish and urged

him to get a regular gardener, instead of having only occasional help.

'You're always behind with the work,' she complained, 'and consequently the garden never looks as nice as it should. And why do you want to bother with growing vegetables? It's easier to get them at the supermarket.'

Max shrugged and did not attempt to explain the satisfaction that was derived from picking and eating his own home-grown lettuces or broccoli. Maybe they weren't up to the standard of those obtainable at the shop, but they were *his*.

Today he dug steadily for some time, returned to the house for bread and cheese, then went back to work. The vegetable patch, which had been in partial shade during the morning, was now in full sun, and the thought of stretching out in a comfortable garden chair suddenly became very attractive. He stuck his spade in the earth, mopped his face and began to stroll slowly up the winding path at the side of the lawn, pausing every now and then to pull out a weed.

For most of the way his eyes were on the ground. When he did eventually look up he halted abruptly and stood staring in amazement.

The house was old and rambling, having once been a farmhouse. There was a courtyard at the back, with outbuildings all round. Standing in the middle and staring about her, apparently unaware of his approach, was a girl.

For a split second he thought Rachel had returned unexpectedly, but his sister's hair was leaf-brown and she wore it cut short. This girl had fair hair hanging round her shoulders. In blank astonishment Max recognised the new nurse.

Fiona had set out with high hopes for her trip down memory lane. Walking up the High Street, she had enjoyed being greeted by people doing their Saturday afternoon shopping. Very few of them were known to her, but she suspected they were all aware of her identity. Passing the old people's flats, she spared a thought for Miss Pennington, now recovering from her operation, and then reached the end of the village, where she came to a sudden halt.

Unless her memory was at fault, there should be a lane here, winding between high hedges towards a house standing alone among fields—the house called Cornerways—and then on to a distant farm. Now the lane had become a properly paved road, with hedges no more than two feet high, and further along a row of ugly new houses had been built.

Fiona nearly turned back, but determination drove her on. She would discover what the passage of time had done to the house of her dreams and then forget it—if she could. Resolutely, she followed the winding road, along which she had so often ridden her bicycle in the past, and the further she walked the more ridiculous became the flights of fancy in which she had recently indulged. A house looking just the same, its kind owners in the garden all ready to invite her in and show her round. It wouldn't be like that at all.

It wasn't.

At first she hardly recognised it. The climbing roses which had scrambled all over the front had vanished, and so had the lavender hedge which had filled the air

with sweetness when her eager young legs had brushed
against it. The front garden was now paved, with prim-
looking plants in tubs dotted about, and there was no
sign of life.

She hesitated by the gate, then marched up to the
front door. She would see if anyone was at home and,
if not, explore a little further before retreating—just in
case the back wasn't quite as bad as the front.

No one answered the bell, though she rang twice.
Feeling horribly like a trespasser—which she was—
Fiona walked round the house and found the courtyard. Delighted, she stood still and stared at it. There
were no kittens, or foraging hens, or any living crea-
tures, but otherwise there seemed little change, and the
wide open door of an outhouse showed an interior
which was positively untidy with garden equipment.

Perhaps the garden would be recognisable too. Fiona
turned round to look at it and found a man standing
there, staring at her.

'What the hell are you doing here?' demanded Max.

The shock was so great that for a moment she was
incapable of speech. But she managed to hold her head
high and meet his astonished gaze.

'I'm sorry,' she said when she had found her voice. 'I
know I haven't any right to be here, but I did ring the
bell and——'

'You had a perfect right to walk round the house
when no one answered the door. I presume you were
looking for me and thought I might be in the garden.'

'No, of course not!' Seeing that she had startled him
afresh, she stumbled on, 'I had no idea you were likely
to be here, so how could I be looking for you?'

'But you must have had *some* reason for coming,' he pointed out.

He was now standing only a couple of yards away, and Fiona was suddenly very much aware of his proximity. Tall and broad and lightly tanned, his reddish hair gleaming in the sun, he made her think of a Viking. Tartly, she reminded herself that Vikings were unlikely to have worn shorts, and produced an answer to his question.

'Of course I had a reason, but it wouldn't interest you, and it doesn't matter anyway.'

She could see that she had intrigued him, though that had certainly not been her intention. He came right up to her and put an earth-stained hand on her arm, causing a most unwelcome tingling sensation.

'I shan't let you go until you've come in the house and given an account of yourself. I can also provide you with a drink, or even a cup of tea if you'd prefer that. You look to me as though you could do with a reviver.'

It was quite true that Fiona was hot, though her flushed cheeks were not entirely due to walking on a warm afternoon. Besides, it would be crazy to throw away this chance of seeing inside the house.

'Thank you,' she said politely. 'That would be very nice, but it's more than I deserve after invading your domain like this.'

He smiled. 'That depends on how interesting your excuse is.'

'It was a reason, not an excuse,' she retorted.

'Have it your own way.' Max opened the kitchen door and ushered her in.

She stopped abruptly on the threshold. The kitchen

had altered out of all recognition. She remembered it as a typical farmhouse kitchen, even though the house had ceased to be a farm, with a big scrubbed table, a dresser loaded with colourful plates, and an Aga giving a gloriously warm welcome to everybody who entered.

Now, completely refitted and the Aga gone, it had a tidiness and cleanliness which was clinical rather than welcoming.

Max, leading the way, had not noticed her reaction, and she quickly pulled herself together and followed him into the big central hall. This was not so much altered, but the sitting-room into which he led her looked as though it had been lifted bodily from the Ideal Home Exhibition. Modern décor in very pale shades, no clutter, not even books, and huge, chunky chairs in soft cream leather.

'Sit down,' he ordered, 'and I'll rustle up drinks. I'm going to have a lager. What would you like?'

'Anything non-alcoholic which happens to be handy.' She spoke as though in a trance, staring round.

Max gave her a puzzled look and busied himself at a side-table. Finding a glass of pineapple juice in her hand a moment later, Fiona sat down and pulled herself together.

'Now,' he said when he had quenched his thirst, 'I want to know what this is all about. I don't flatter myself you called here to see me.'

'I told you I had no idea you lived here.'

'Or you wouldn't have come?'

'Of course not.' Hastily, she added, 'I wouldn't have had any reason for calling on you.'

He grinned. 'Not very flattering, but I'll let it pass. Why *did* you come?'

Fiona told him, speaking in jerks and trying to make it sound casual when it very obviously wasn't. Max listened without interruption, sipping his drink and staring out at the sunlit garden. When she had finished he sat for a moment in silence, apparently thinking over what he had been told. Glad that her confession was over, Fiona relaxed and leaned back in the chair.

'Is that all?' he asked at last.

She started and her fingers tightened on the glass as some of her tension returned. 'Isn't it enough?'

'I don't think it is. Such a fixation on the past seems to me rather unhealthy.'

'I haven't got a fixation!' she said indignantly.

'I believe you have.' Seeing her about to interrupt, he held up an imperious hand. 'I admit there's nothing particularly strange about wanting to see again a house which has left you with such happy memories, but the way you told it gave me the distinct impression it means more to you than it should.'

'If I'd known you were an amateur psychiatrist I wouldn't have told you. I only did it because I thought you were entitled to some explanation.'

'How old are you?' Max demanded, ignoring her angry comment.

'If you must know, I'm twenty-four. Why?'

'At your age you should either be enjoying the present or looking forward to the future. Why aren't you?'

Fiona was so furious she jumped to her feet and stood in the middle of the pale honey-coloured carpet, glaring down at him. 'My future is my own affair, and I wish I could say the same of my present. Unfortunately you're also involved with that to a certain extent, but it doesn't give you the right to question me and invade my privacy.'

Max leaned back against the soft cream leather and looked up at her with half-closed eyes. 'Come down off your high horse and let me take you out to dinner,' he suggested lazily.

'Out to dinner?' she gasped. 'I—I wouldn't go out to dinner with you if—if you were the last man on earth!'

He laughed outright. 'Can't you think of anything more original than that?' he mocked.

Completely deflated, Fiona turned away in despair. The next thing she knew he was out of his chair and had taken her by the shoulders, gently but firmly twisting her round to face him.

'If I promise not to catechise you any more, will you come?'

A quite inexplicable temptation immediately assailed her. She had nothing else lined up for the rest of the day and Liz had gone to Easterwood to visit her aged mother. It would be nice to have somebody to talk to, even if they did keep sparring.

'I'm not dressed for going out to dinner,' she protested, looking down at her jeans.

'I wasn't suggesting the Ritz, but there are some very good pubs around here where you can get meals. All that's necessary is for me to change out of my gardening clothes and make myself look clean and tidy. No problem, I assure you.'

'You certainly don't fit in with the house at the moment,' she agreed, looking him up and down, her eyes pausing momentarily on his muscular thighs.

He paused with his hand on the door-knob. 'Is that

why you don't like the house as it is now? Too clean and tidy?'

'I didn't say I didn't like it.'

'My dear girl, a complete moron would have guessed it compared very unfavourably with the way it was in your grandparents' day.'

'I wouldn't have known it was the same place,' she said sadly. 'It's all been brought so dreadfully up to date.'

'That was my sister's doing.' Max leaned back against the wall with his arms folded, prepared for further conversation. 'The house belongs to my parents, not to me. They bought it for their retirement and my sister, who's into interior decorating, did it up for them. I'm not sure they liked it any more than you do. Anyway, they'd no sooner moved here than my father developed a serious bronchitic condition and they went off to live in Spain for a while. It happened just about the time I joined the practice. Very convenient for me, but sad for them.'

'Does your sister live here too?' Fiona asked, thinking of that clinical kitchen. No man could ever have kept it like that.

'Most of the time, but she's away this weekend. When her marriage started to fall apart she had a bit of a breakdown, so I thought I'd better keep an eye on her.'

Fiona was touched by his care for his sister, and then she realised he had probably benefited even more than the girl. It must be very useful to have a sort of built-in housekeeper. 'Has she any children?' she asked.

Max shook his head. 'I'm inclined to think it's a good

thing. Kids are usually the ones to suffer most in a divorce.'

'You can say that again!' Fiona exclaimed before she could stop herself.

Max immediately pounced on the remark. 'Will you tell me off for prying if I dare to ask whether you have personal experience of people divorcing?'

'My parents parted when I was ten.'

'And was that when you stopped coming to Tarling for your holidays?'

'Yes,' she said curtly, and left it at that.

Even if her father's parents had not been killed in that awful accident, she doubted whether her mother would have made it convenient for her to visit them again. A successful businesswoman, she had brought her only child up conscientiously, but as soon as Fiona had been launched into nursing she had moved into a one-bedroom flat in an expensive part of London. She had not actually said, 'You're on your own now,' but the implication had been clear enough. Fiona had not spent another night under her roof and hoped she never would.

As she sat waiting in the sitting-room while sounds of running water drifted down the stairs, she heard a shout.

'Which was your room when you stayed here?'

'The little one looking out over the garden,' she called back.

'Like to come up and see it? You might find it fits in better with your memories than the rest of the house.'

Fiona scarcely hesitated. When she was halfway up the stairs, she said, 'I thought you didn't approve of nostalgia.'

'I don't, but I'm willing to stretch a point in a good cause.'

His voice was now quite near, and she looked up to see him standing on the landing. He had evidently been taking a shower and was wearing a short terry-towelling robe and—probably—nothing else. His wet tawny hair stood up all over his head and his bare chest gleamed with a plentiful supply of red-gold curls. His strong neck, smooth and young-looking, supported his well-shaped head with unconscious arrogance.

Finding the sight of so much masculine virility strangely disturbing, Fiona droopeed her eyes and then had to wrench her gaze away again as she discovered his bare legs had as devastating an effect on her as the rest of him.

She had an uneasy feeling that he knew exactly what he was doing to her.

'Why did you say I might find my old room less changed than anywhere else?' she asked a little breathlessly.

'Because it escaped Rachel's decorating efforts and I think it's probably always been a child's room. Come and see.'

He opened a door at the end of the passage, and Fiona squeezed past him. One look round told her he was right. The wallpaper wasn't the one she remembered, but it was the same type—tiny pink roses on a white ground, pretty, girlish and old-fashioned. The cupboard and bookcase, both built-in, were still painted white, and the view of the garden was dominated by a huge cedar, just as it had always been.

She stood still by the window and, to her horror, felt tears welling up into her eyes. Max was obviously waiting for her to say something, but she felt choked by emotion and utterly incapable of words. She stared out, blinking furiously and willing him to go away and leave her alone to recover her composure.

But instead of that he came up behind her and touched her bowed head, stroking the silky golden hair with a gentle hand. Instead of the abrasive comment she expected, he asked casually, 'Why don't you wear your hair loose like this all the time? It completely alters your image.'

Chris had asked that question, and she had explained that a nurse wearing the uniform of St Martin's was expected to look trim and efficient, not sexy. She tried to give Max the same answer and found speech impossible. Putting both hands over her face, she burst into tears.

'Good God!' Max wrapped strong, comforting arms round her slender body, which was shaking with sobs, and held her close. 'Whoever would have thought the cool, calm and collected Nurse Shelton could carry on like this?'

'I'm—sorry!' Fiona gasped.

'Don't apologise. I'm finding it extremely interesting. Nothing will convince me you're crying just because your old room looks much the same as you remember it. I would have thought that would cause pleasure rather than tears.'

He paused and then, receiving no reply, went on thoughtfully, 'Nor do I think the fact that you come from a broken home is an adequate cause either. I believe there's another reason for all this distress—something much more recent. Am I right?'

By a superhuman effort Fiona regained control. She

twisted round in his embrace and said in a voice made husky by emotion but none the less firm, 'You're catechising me again. I thought we agreed——'

'So we did, but I can't help finding you extremely intriguing and I'm afraid I'm likely to forget myself now and again. Unless, of course, you'd care to tell me all about it now?'

'I most certainly would not!' she snapped.

'So you admit there's something else to tell?'

'I admit nothing.'

'OK, I give in, for the present anyway.' He put one finger under her chin and tilted her face upwards, looking at her critically. 'Those big brown eyes of yours, which make such a fetching contrast with your blonde hair, look as though they could do with being bathed in cold water. So I suggest you give your mind to restoring your appearance in order to make yourself fit to come out to supper with me, and while you're doing that I'll dress.'

He bent his head swiftly and kissed her on the mouth, his lips cool and firm. Before she could protest he said cheerfully, 'See you!' and went off to his room.

In a daze Fiona made her way to the bathroom. She scarcely noticed that the plain white suite she remembered had been replaced by an avocado one which included a bidet. She was too busy trying to make herself look 'fit to come out to supper'. Somehow, it seemed to have become rather important.

CHAPTER FOUR

THE restaurant at the White Hart at Bedgrave was candlelit and pleasantly withdrawn from the noise of the bars. It was mostly occupied by couples of varying ages, and Fiona guessed it was a popular place for Saturday meals out. The quiet murmur of conversation suggested people were enjoying themselves in a low-key kind of way.

Slowly and at first imperceptibly the atmosphere wrapped her round, until she too began to be aware of taking pleasure in her surroundings, the simple but perfectly cooked food—and even in her companion. Until they began to talk about reflexology.

'Why are you so against it?' Fiona demanded, fixing Max with a challenging stare across the table.

'Because it's completely phoney,' he said promptly, leaning across and refilling her glass. 'You'll have to drink most of the bottle, because I'm driving.'

Normally Fiona was extremely careful about alcohol, having seen the results of over-indulgence when she was working in the accident unit. But she was so much in earnest now that she scarcely noticed that her glass glowed red all the way up. 'I don't see you've got any right to call it phoney when there are so many people who have been helped by the treatment.'

'Who says they have?'

'Why, Liz, of course——'

'She's the last person you ought to ask about it.

Obviously she'd make out she'd been successful, partly because she's dead keen about it but also because her living depends on it.'

Fiona's brown eyes glowed with dark, smouldering fire. 'So you're making out she's a liar?'

'Of course I'm not! I wasn't in Tarling when Liz Crane was the surgery nurse, but I've never heard anything but praise of her work and general character. But there's such a thing as wishful thinking, and I reckon that's what she's suffering from now. All this reflexology lark is utter rubbish.'

'Dr McBride doesn't call it that,' Fiona argued.

Max shrugged and took a sip of wine. 'He's past the crusading age and likes a quiet life, in addition to which he's got a kind heart. He knows reflexology can't do any harm and so he lets Liz get on with it.' With an air of great magnanimity he added, 'It's even possible she does occasionally do some good with the type of patients who are easily influenced psychologically.'

If only Liz herself were here, Fiona reflected, she would know how to answer him and disprove his chauvinistic assertions. It would do him good to be taken down a peg or two—nobody had any right to be as sure of himself as Max Whitmore!

'Are you against all forms of alternative medicine?' she asked.

He frowned, giving the question his serious consideration. 'I think osteopaths do a good job,' he admitted eventually.

'Yet at one time doctors didn't approve of them either, or so I've been told.'

'The medical profession,' Max declared, 'must always be cautious about adopting anything new. It has to be. After all, it's responsible for people's lives and it couldn't possibly lend its support to every daft new treatment that comes along.'

Her eyes twinkled wickedly. 'You sounded just as though you were making a speech.'

'What?' He glared at her indignantly.

For a moment she thought she was going to have a demonstration of his by now well-known temper. But he controlled himself and laughed instead.

'Why are we having such a ridiculously solemn conversation?' he enquired.

'I can't imagine. What shall we talk about instead?'

Max leaned across the table, his eyes on her face. 'The most interesting subject I can think of is—*you*.'

'Me?' She flinched and then tried to hide it by a forced lightness. 'You could hardly have suggested a more boring subject.'

'It might be boring to you because you know it all. I feel quite sure I would find it fascinating.' He tried to hold her gaze, but she defeated him by looking down at her plate.

'Then I'm afraid you'll have to remain un-fascinated.' A flash of inspiration came out of the blue. 'Tell me about your work as an accident doctor. I'm sure that really would be interesting.'

He looked surprised. 'I didn't know you were even aware of it.'

'Of course I'm aware of it.' She couldn't resist the temptation to tease him. 'I was involved in it once.'

'You what?'

'Do you remember that head-on collision between a Mini and a Volvo not very far away from here? I was the girl who loomed up out of the darkness and offered to help, only to get my head bitten off by the doctor in charge.'

'Good God!' His dismay was so brief Fiona only just glimpsed it before he rallied. 'You can't blame me for not recognising you when you turned up at the surgery looking totally different—and in any case, I didn't really see you properly that night. You were just somebody offering help, and I was grateful.'

Her skilfully darkened brows rose in astonishment. 'Grateful? *You*! You told me to get the hell out of it and——'

'That must have been before I knew you were a nurse.'

Fiona was obliged to admit he was right about that, but she swiftly returned to the attack. 'Even when I said I was a nurse you continued to be exceedingly rude. If it hadn't been for the passenger needing my help I wouldn't have stayed.'

Max leaned back in his chair, his arms folded and a brooding look on his face. 'I rather get the impression,' he said at last, 'that you don't much care for me. Am I right?'

Emboldened by the wine she had drunk, Fiona opened her mouth to tell him he was perfectly right, then inexplicably closed it again because she had suddenly realised he wasn't quite as much right as she had thought. Slightly muddled, she groped for an answer which would be the truth and yet not too condemnatory. After all, he had been kind to her when she'd made such a fool of herself at Cornerways, and she was enjoying being taken out to supper.

'There are times when I don't like you at all,' she said carefully. 'Quite a lot of times, in fact. But

sometimes you're completely different, like now. I
don't know which is the real you.'

Max was looking thunderstruck, and she wondered if
anybody had ever spoken to him like that before. She
supposed she ought to apologise for her plain speaking,
but she really couldn't be bothered. Dreamily, she
picked up her glass and drank a little more wine.

'*In vino veritas*,' he said suddenly with a grin.

Fiona blinked at him. 'I was never much good at
Latin.'

'It means that people are more likely to be truthful
when they've been drinking than when they're sober.'

'How dare you suggest I'm not perfectly sober?'

'I was only copying your own plain speaking,' he
pointed out, his eyes dancing.

Toying with the remains of a roll on her side plate,
she tried to think of a telling reply, but was unable to
produce one. Perhaps it was a fact that she was not
entirely sober? She usually drank so little that it was
possible the very moderate amount of wine she had
had might have affected her more than it would someone accustomed to it.

'Did the Mini driver survive?' she asked, to change
the subject.

His expression altered. 'Yes—up to a point,' he said
curtly.

'What do you mean? He's either alive or he isn't.'

'That's a matter of opinion. Technically he's alive
because he's still breathing, but it's only with the aid of
a life support machine. Personally, I consider that a
living death.'

Fiona leaned forward earnestly. 'Have you never
heard of that grotty old saying, "While there's life

there's hope"? It's true, you know. Miracles are constantly happening in hospital.'

'I certainly wouldn't challenge you on that,' he admitted.

There was a slightly uncomfortable silence as both of them became aware they had strayed into deep waters. It was a relief when the waitress appeared with their coffee. By the time she had drunk her share of the generous-sized pot, Fiona was glad to find she was quite herself again. Sheltering behind her normal reserve, she thanked Max politely for a delicious meal and they went out to the car park.

They did not speak during the short drive back to Tarling. Fiona's mind was busy with a practical problem. It would be normal behaviour to ask him in for coffee, but it was Liz's house and she might not welcome someone who so much disapproved of her profession, even though she liked him personally. On the other hand, she might not be there, since she had said it was possible she would spend the night with her mother.

But if that were the case, it made the situation even more difficult. Fiona was not at all sure she wanted to be alone with a man whose personality affected her so deplorably.

They arrived at Apple Acre without her being aware of having taken any decision, but her mind seemed to have settled the matter on its own, for, as soon as she had ascertained that the house was in darkness, she heard herself suggesting coffee.

'That would be very nice,' Max said politely, 'but perhaps Miss Crane——'

'I think she's spending the night in Easterwood.'

'I see,' he said thoughtfully. 'In that case I'll certainly accept.'

What exactly did he think he saw? Scarlet with embarrassment, Fiona got out and walked ahead of him up the path. Inside the house, she switched on an unnecessary number of lights and, murmuring something about the kettle, started off for the kitchen.

'Do we really need any more coffee?' Max called after her. 'We got through about a gallon at the pub.'

'What would you like instead, then?'

'Do I have to have anything? Can't we just sit down and—talk?'

'We've been talking for hours,' she pointed out hurriedly.

'I expect there's plenty that hasn't yet been said.' He followed her down the passage and put his hand on her bare arm. 'Stop being a hostess, Fiona, and come and be sociable instead.'

Her heart was thudding as she allowed him to lead her back to the sitting-room, but, once there, she wrenched herself free. How could she get it into his head that the cosy session he obviously had in mind was definitely not on? And what had happened to her usual poise? Why did she feel like a schoolgirl out on her first date?

Rescue came from a totally unexpected quarter. A car door slammed outside and footsteps came up the path. As she heard a key being fitted in the lock, Fiona knew it must be Liz.

Standing in the open doorway of the sitting-room, she found herself saying stupidly, 'I thought you must have decided to stay the night,' and cringed as she realised the interpretation which could be put on it.

'I wanted to, but my mother is very independent and she wouldn't hear of it, so I saw her into bed and then came back.' Glancing past Fiona, Liz raised her eyebrows slightly and said a cool, 'Hello, Doctor. How are you?'

'Fine.' Max had risen to his feet politely. 'Just going anyway, as a matter of fact.'

'Don't let me frighten you away.' Liz turned towards the kitchen. 'I'm urgently needing coffee. Like some?'

'No, thanks.'

'I'll say goodnight, then.' Calling her dog, Liz continued on her way.

Fiona went with Max to the front door, intending to say an equally brief farewell, but before she realised what was happening she found herself on the wrong side of an almost-closed door. As she made a small sound of protest, his arms enveloped her and her lips were silenced by the urgent demand of his mouth. Dazed and helpless, she allowed her body to relax against his, and all the bitterness and frustration of the last few months found relief in an upsurge of passionate emotion.

The kiss lasted a long time, but at last Max raised his head and looked down into her eyes. In the light from the hall she could see that his were dancing.

'I thought there was something very different hidden beneath that ice-cold "touch me not" look of yours,' he murmured. 'I was right, wasn't I?'

'I don't know what you mean,' Fiona hedged.

'You know perfectly well.' He paused, his face suddenly serious. 'Who was the guy who taught you to kiss like that? He must have meant a lot to you.'

She was flung into an instant panic. 'You've no right

to ask me that sort of question! Anyway, what makes you think anybody taught me? I thought it was just an ordinary goodnight kiss.'

'Liar,' he said softly in her ear, his lips nuzzling a tendril of pale gold hair. 'You know darned well it was something different. I don't flatter myself it was because of me, so what was it?'

Fiona's brain worked furiously. Perhaps if she told him a little, he would stop plaguing her. 'If you must know——' she tried to speak lightly '—my tutor was a doctor at the same hospital. For a time we believed we had something really good going for us, but we were wrong. That's all.'

It was far from being all. For one thing, only one of them had been wrong—Chris. She had not stopped loving him just because he had chosen someone else; she had continued to feel her love for him had been special, and therein lay the heartbreak.

'Poor Fiona.' Max kissed her gently. 'Was that why you resigned from hospital nursing and came to Tarling?'

She shrugged. 'Partly, I suppose, but I felt I wanted a change for all sorts of reasons. You already know about one of them—I wanted to make contact with my roots.' Suddenly she knew she had had enough, and she finished hurriedly, 'I really must go in. Liz will wonder what on earth——'

He laughed. 'She's not that daft! But I guess it's time I went, all the same. Thanks for your company, Fiona. By and large, it's been quite an interesting day.'

Safely indoors, Fiona closed the door carefully and went with some reluctance to find Liz, who was sitting at the kitchen table, sipping her coffee. She looked up with a grin.

'Sorry if I interrupted anything.'

'Of course you didn't.' Fiona sat down opposite and launched into an account of her afternoon and evening. 'It was an awful shock finding the Whitmores lived at my grandparents' house,' she said when she had finished the bald account.

'My dear, life's full of coincidences of that sort.' Liz looked at her thoughtfully across the top of her mug. 'Somehow I get the impression you don't dislike that young man as much as you did. A week ago you were describing him as a male chauvinist pig, and you certainly wouldn't have dreamt of going out to dinner with him.'

'I've discovered he's got another side, that's all,' Fiona declared nonchalantly.

'I told you the patients liked him. After all, people are very rarely the same all through like that seaside rock we used to buy when I was a child.' Liz hesitated, her eyes narrowing as she studied her lodger. 'Take yourself, for instance,' she went on. 'I wouldn't mind betting you're quite different sometimes from the cool, professional Nurse Shelton who appears at the surgery. Like this evening.' Her eyes glinting wickedly, she waited for Fiona's reaction.

Twice inside fifteen minutes was really too much, and Fiona was fed up with being analysed. How could she ever have been so foolish as to imagine that in Tarling she would be able to remain completely withdrawn, her unhappy secret intact? She'd only been here a week and already Max knew something about her childhood and—much worse—he had become aware of the existence of Chris. Well, she wasn't going to tell Liz, much as she liked her. And so she just smiled and announced that she was off to bed.

Sunday was a quiet day, which should have soothed Fiona's restless mind but failed to do so. She took the dog for a long walk, which tired her physically but not enough to ensure a good night's sleep. The result was that the alarm woke her with a jerk and she started the week with a headache. Fortunately the short walk to the surgery soon banished it, and she arrived on duty feeling her normal self. Or very nearly. The memory of how she had responded to Max's kiss was still there at the back of her mind, ready to thrust itself forward and worry her at the first opportunity.

To her surprise, she found Dr David Kennedy waiting to see her. So far she had not had much to do with this quiet, unobtrusive young widower. He was slightly built and not much taller than Fiona, with dark eyes and dark brown hair. He would, she supposed, be quite attractive if he looked more cheerful.

Not that anyone could blame him for looking depressed, she hastily reminded herself. It was only eighteen months since his wife had died of leukaemia, leaving him with two small children.

This morning he produced a pleasant smile which remained totally impersonal. 'I wanted to see you, Nurse, before going over to Bedgrave,' he told Fiona.

'What can I do for you?' she asked.

'It's about my mother-in-law.' Seeing her involuntary look of surprise, he added hastily, 'Nothing to do with all those silly jokes! I'm deeply grateful to her—she's taken charge of my house and looked after my children ever since Mary died. She's a truly wonderful woman, I assure you.'

'What exactly is worrying you?'

'She's a very keen gardener, but she's never had any anti-tetanus jabs. I'm anxious that she should get herself protected, but unfortunately she's one of those people who dread an injection. I've just made an appointment for her to come here and have the first inoculation——'

'Do you think she'll come?'

'Oh, yes. She's a very sensible person and knows she shouldn't give in to that sort of irrational fear. I'm only mentioning it so that you're forewarned and can take that little bit of extra trouble with her.'

He needn't have bothered, Fiona reflected. She would almost certainly have guessed how the patient was feeling the moment she entered the room, but it was nice of him, all the same. Aloud, she asked for his mother-in-law's name, and was told it was Mrs Janet Forbes.

'Does she realise she'll need three injections spaced over about six months?' she asked.

He looked alarmed. 'Oh, no, I haven't told her that. I thought it would—er—sound better coming from you.' And with another of his strangely blank smiles he went off to Bedgrave.

Typical male! she thought wryly, and went to ask Anne when to expect Mrs Forbes. It turned out to be the following afternoon.

'She's ever such a nice lady and looks after those kids as though she were their mum instead of their nana,' the receptionist said. 'I don't know what she'll do when David marries again.'

'Has he got somebody in view?'

'If he has, he's been keeping it very quiet, and that's not easy in Tarling. I was only thinking he's almost sure to marry somebody eventually. I mean, he's not *that* old—not much more than thirty, I should think.'

Chris had been thirty, and Fiona had always thought of it as the perfect age for marriage as far as the man was concerned. How old was Max? she wondered, and wasted several seconds trying to make up her mind. Eventually she concluded that he must be about the same age. Disgusted with herself for such a pointless activity, she got down to work.

When Mrs Forbes arrived the following day, Fiona looked at her with interest, and immediately detected the tenseness she was trying to hide.

Janet Forbes was quite frank about her phobia. 'I know it's silly,' she apologised, 'but I've always dreaded the needle.'

'A lot of people feel like that about it. I don't suppose you'll believe me when I tell you it's not nearly as painful as pricking yourself when you're sewing, but it's true—unless, of course, the nurse or doctor is clumsy with the hypodermic, and I assure you I'm *very* experienced.'

Fiona began to chat about the patient's grand-children, asking their names and ages, and soon had her talking naturally. 'Dr Kennedy is very lucky to have you to help him,' she said warmly, 'but I expect you enjoy it. I mean, of course, apart from the reason for your having to be here.'

A shadow crossed Mrs Forbes's attractive, carefully made-up face. 'I adore those children, Nurse, and yet— well, I always meant to travel after my husband died.

He'd been an invalid for many years and I knew I would lose him eventually. It happened not long before Mary—my daughter—had to give up her fight with leukaemia.'

'Oh, dear—that must have been dreadful for you!' Fiona exclaimed, not at all sure she had done the right thing in starting all this.

It had had one good effect, though. Mrs Forbes had scarcely noticed the injection.

'Yes, it was, but I'm tough and I've survived. I sometimes think I've coped better than poor David. He seems to be stuck in a slough of despond, though I must say he makes an effort when he's with the children.'

When she had gone, Fiona sat for a moment thinking over their conversation. A short while ago she had never even seen Janet Forbes. Now she felt she knew her quite well and liked everything about her. It was impossible not to be sympathetic over the way she had got herself trapped in a domestic situation which looked like going on for years unless her son-in-law married again.

Later on, as she tidied her room preparatory to leaving, Fiona reflected with some satisfaction that she had not seen Max all day. He had been working at Bedgrave with David Kennedy, and presumably had had no occasion to call in at the Tarling surgery. Yesterday, too, they hadn't exchanged more than a few words. The two quietly busy days had gone a long way towards restoring her to a more sensible frame of mind, and in future her relations with Max Whitmore would be strictly professional.

She was closing the outer door behind her when a

woman aged about fifty came hurrying into view. She was wearing an apron and looked as though she had dashed out of the house without stopping to tidy herself.

Fiona halted automatically. 'Can I help you?'

'Are any of the doctors in?'

'Not yet. It should be Dr McBride and his daughter, but they've both been delayed. Is there something I can do, Mrs—er——?'

'Dale is the name, but it's my neighbour I'm concerned about. My husband and I've been away to Easterwood to spend a long weekend with our daughter—only just got back. He dropped me at our cottage and went off to the garage to get something done to the car, and I suddenly noticed there was a pint of milk on the step next door. That'd be Monday's pint. Miss Tanner only has three pints a week, seeing as she's on her own, so there's isn't another one due till tomorrow——' She paused for breath and pushed back some wisps of hair from her hot face.

'You think Miss Tanner has been taken ill?'

'It's worse than that. I didn't do anything at first, but it bothered me all the time I was laying the table for tea, and I decided to nip round and peep in the kitchen window.' She paused for dramatic effect. 'The poor old lady's lying there on the kitchen floor.'

'Is there any means of getting in?' Fiona asked sharply.

'The door wasn't locked.' A slightly ashamed look appeared on Mrs Dale's face. 'I didn't like to go in, not by myself, so will you come, please, Nurse?'

They set off without further discussion and saved their breath for walking quickly. It was a very short distance and, arrived at Miss Tanner's cottage, Fiona went straight down the narrow side-passage and, her heart beating a little faster, opened the back door.

It had been a cool, showery day and the little house was as cold and damp as a cellar. The floor was bare tiles and the old lady stretched out on it was only wearing a nightdress and dressing-gown, both of which had rucked up when she fell so that her blue-veined legs stuck out grotesquely. At first Fiona thought she was dead, but her searching fingers detected a faint pulse.

'She's suffering severely from hypothermia,' she said, 'and I wouldn't be surprised if she's broken her hip-bone, but the cold is the more serious——'

'Shall I fetch a hot-water bottle?' Mrs Dale offered eagerly.

'No, thank you. She must be warmed up only very gradually. If you've got a light blanket, I'd be grateful if you would tuck it round her while I dash back to the surgery and see if a doctor has arrived.'

There were three cars there, and one of them was Max's. He was standing at the reception counter when Fiona hurried in, his fingers tapping impatiently while some information was searched for. He turned in surprise when she accosted him. Gasping, she gave him a brief outline of the story.

'Miss Tanner's one of my patients, so I'd better take a look at her.' Briskly, he asked for an ambulance to be requested and then turned back to Fiona. 'You come with me,' he ordered.

Sitting beside him, she had just time to feel glad that the journey was so short, and her concern for Miss Tanner was sufficient to keep other more unruly

thoughts at bay. If only it could always be like this—a
friendly but entirely professional relationship—there
would be no problem.

She must do her utmost to keep it that way—she
really *must*!

Mrs Dale had followed her instructions carefully and
Max removed the blanket only briefly to conduct a
quick examination. He confirmed Fiona's guess that
the hip was broken and instructed her to remain with
the patient until the ambulance arrived.

'I must be off—I've got a lot of visits to make.' He
paused in the doorway to bestow a charming smile on
Mrs Dale. 'Your neighbourly concern has probably
saved the old lady's life,' he told her warmly.

She received the compliment with a girlish simper.
'He's ever such a nice young man, isn't he?' she said
when he had gone.

Was he? Fiona still wasn't really sure.

CHAPTER FIVE

THE London train was late and Max stood waiting impatiently at Easterwood station. He had promised his sister he would meet her when she returned from her weekend away because, otherwise, she would have to take a taxi, which would be expensive. Since the break-up of her marriage and consequent inability to work she had not been able to afford extravagances.

This visit to London had been an experiment. It was her first since her partial recovery and he was anxious to know how she had got on. She had been staying with old friends, and seeing them again would have aroused painful memories with which she might not be able to cope.

Once glance at her face when the train eventually arrived told him she was feeling tensed up, but she seemed to have herself under control. They walked down the platform together, the girl taking short, quick steps. She was not very tall and extremely thin, with a pale skin and wispy leaf-brown hair. No one would have taken them for brother and sister.

'I hope I haven't made you late with your evening calls,' Rachel said anxiously.

'Not seriously.' Max took her elbow and steered her towards his car.

When they had left the worst of the traffic behind them he asked the all-important question. 'How did it go?'

'I enjoyed the theatre,' she said brightly in her high, brittle voice. 'I'm not so sure about the rest of the weekend and I don't want to go again just yet, but— well, I'm glad I made the effort.'

That, at least, was something. To divert her, he began to talk about Fiona's visit to Cornerways and the reason for it. Rachel's interest was immediately caught, as he had hoped it would be.

'That's fascinating, Max! I'd very much like to meet this girl. There's a lot she could tell me about the house as it used to be, and I'm sure I'd find it interesting.'

'I don't think she approved of your decorative scheme,' he warned her.

'Oh! Well, I suppose she's got this very clear memory of Cornerways in her mind and she probably wouldn't like *any* alterations. We must make allowances.' Rachel groped in her bag for a cigarette and held it unlit in her hand as she glanced at him. 'May I?'

'*Must* you?'

'I've kept off them all the weekend, but I'm absolutely gasping for one now, Max darling. *Please* don't say I can't have just this one!'

He sighed and pulled out the ashtray. 'Go ahead, if you're that desperate.'

She lit it quickly and drew the smoke deeply into her lungs. When she'd first come to live with her brother she had been smoking fifty a day. Between them, they had got it down to one only occasionally, which was a considerable achievement.

Max made no further comment, but he knew his disapproval must be almost a tangible thing between them and that Rachel was only too conscious of it. She probably wouldn't really enjoy the cigarette, and serve her right! He had smoked surreptitiously at school and then decided it was a mug's game. It was quite impossible for him to understand some people's need, and he had, for him, been incredibly patient with Rachel's addiction.

'Let's ask Fiona to a meal,' she suggested when she had disposed of the stub. 'When's your day off this week?'

'I'm not sure. Maggie said something about wanting to change with me, but she didn't confirm it, but you could ask Fiona at a weekend. I'm only on call then.'

'You might have to go dashing off.'

'And I might not.'

'OK, then, we'll ask her to supper next weekend. Will you fix it?'

'If that's what you want.' Rachel nodded vigorously and he patted her arm in an elder-brotherly kind of way. 'I'm very glad you feel like entertaining. It's a great step forward.'

He issued the invitation the next day, making it sound very careless and casual. 'My sister wants you to tell her all about the house and thinks it should be done over a meal, so I received instructions to invite you to supper. Either Saturday or Sunday.'

Fiona looked at him in astonishment. 'I'm sure I can't tell her anything she would find interesting.'

'Rachel seems to think you can. Which evening would you prefer?'

He had taken it for granted she would be free to accept, Fiona thought crossly, and felt very tempted to refuse. But it would be difficult to think up an excuse and, besides, she was not *really* sure she wanted to refuse.

'I might go out for the day on Sunday,' she told him, improvising rapidly, 'so it had better be Saturday.'

'Right.' On his way out, he paused with his hand on the door-knob. 'I can't tell you how pleased I am about this, Fiona. It's the very first time my sister has felt up to meeting anyone at a social occasion, apart from the old friends she's just been staying with, of course.'

He glanced at her over his shoulder, obviously surprised that she made no comment, and then went out of the room, closing the door behind him.

She sat staring at the door for a moment, extremely cross with herself because she had failed to express her own pleasure in the improvement in Rachel's self-confidence. It really had been churlish to wish Max had phrased the remark differently, that he hadn't so clearly given the impression that 'anyone' would have done.

Nevertheless she couldn't help feeling a little hurt.

On Saturday evening she dressed with care, conscious that her own confidence needed support. Her dress of jade-green silk was very plain but beautifully cut and had been expensive. The long silver earrings were her only ornament, and her freshly shampooed hair gleamed with health.

It was something of a blow to find Rachel in trousers with a dreary-looking fawn check shirt hanging loose, but Max's eyes had told her she was looking attractive, and her spirits rose accordingly.

He was very silent at supper, leaving the two girls to talk to each other, and as Rachel chattered almost continuously about the house, Fiona wondered if he was bored. By the end of the rather inadequate meal—the hostess had forgotten to cook the potatoes—she

felt she had dredged up every tiny memory to feed to
Rachel's insatiable curiosity. If the interrogation went
on much longer she would be tempted to call on her
imagination.

She was rescued by the telephone.

Max went off to answer it, but reappeared after a
very brief conversation. He stood in the doorway,
looking at Fiona. 'Do you feel like helping me with an
accident?'

She was instantly in a panic and, before she could
answer, his sister burst into speech.

'Oh, Max, you can't drag Fiona away and leave me
all alone!'

'Sorry, love.' He came nearer and put his hand on
her shoulder. 'I wouldn't have suggested it if it hadn't
happened to be a school coach that's run into trouble—
kids returning from a trip abroad. The ferry was late
getting into Felixstowe or they'd all have been home
before dark. Somehow there was a collision with a
container lorry arriving for the night's crossing.'

Rachel shuddered. 'Oh, dear—it doesn't sound very
nice.' She glanced at Fiona. 'She can't possibly go with
you wearing that lovely dress!'

Fiona pulled herself together. 'If you could lend me
some jeans——'

'Jeans?' Rachel looked vague. 'I will if I can find
them.'

'You'd better go upstairs with her, Fiona,' Max
ordered. 'And be quick about it. The whole point about
this Rescue Service is that a doctor gets there *quickly*.'

Both girls hurried to obey him and Fiona was back
inside a minute. The jeans were paint-stained, but it
hardly mattered, since before long they might well be

stained with blood; with them she wore a T-shirt, and at the last minute Rachel thrust a shabby anorak into her hand. She felt a mess, but Max gave her an approving glance.

They reached the scene of the crash much sooner than she had expected, and she had scarcely had time to steel herself for what she might see. She had imagined the accident to have taken place near the port, but it turned out to be some distance from it, and both the coach and the lorry had been taking a short cut along a road unsuitable for large vehicles.

The police were doing their best to illuminate the scene, and it was only too easy to see that the coach had suffered much more than the lorry. All one side had been ripped off, resulting in huge quantities of broken glass and the inevitable severe cuts. Children, mostly aged about twelve or thirteen, were crying uncontrollably or just sitting on the grassy bank so frozen with shock that they were incapable of producing any sort of sound.

'I'm going inside,' said Max. 'You take charge of those who've managed to get out.'

Unfortunately three out of the four teachers had been on the damaged side, but a white-faced girl, with one eye rapidly closing but otherwise unhurt, was trying to cope with the children who were more frightened than hurt.

All Fiona's nerves had left her as soon as there was something to do. Max had handed her his emergency kit while he assessed the situation inside the coach and she found everything she needed for temporary bandaging. As she worked her way along the line of children, she became aware of a man sitting at the end, staring into space and muttering to himself intermittently.

'I never had a chance, not a chance. Bloody great lorry shouldn't have been using this road!'

'Are you the driver?' Fiona asked when she reached him.

He looked at her vaguely. ''Sright.'

'Are you hurt?' She looked him over and could see no obvious sign of damage.

'Knocked my head on something, didn't I?'

Her probing fingers soon found a lump and he winced as she touched it. 'I expect the doctor will want you to go to hospital and have this looked at properly.'

Max had emerged from the coach and now came to join her. 'What have we got here?'

'Concussion,' she said briefly. 'The children I've been dealing with have all got minor cuts and bruises, but I expect you'll want to send them to hospital for a check-up. How did you find things inside?'

'Bad, but it might have been worse. Nobody was bleeding to death and there weren't any fatalities. Yes, what is it?' He turned to the young teacher, who was tugging his sleeve.

'I've been counting heads. There's—there's someone missing.'

'What?'

'It's a little girl. Her friend who was sitting next to her says she just vanished. I think she must have gone out of the space where the window had been.'

'But that's impossible! The two vehicles are wedged together and there's no room for anyone to fall out.' Max turned to stare at the mass of metal and wood which blocked the road as completely as though the two parts had been welded into one.

'She must be somewhere,' the teacher said despairingly, 'and I really don't feel I can go into that coach and search for her. The policeman counted them in there for me and I don't think he would make a mistake. There are fifteen inside and twenty-four on the bank, and I can't make that add up to forty.' Her voice trembled and she looked on the verge of collapse.

Fiona took her arm and led her to the side of the road. 'You've been doing marvellously and, now we're here, you can sit down and take a rest.'

Max had been re-checking the casualties inside, and he now reappeared.

'There's nothing wrong with the arithmetic,' he said quietly to Fiona, 'and I think the child probably did go out of the window, if she was sitting at the back. The coach seems to have stopped when its last two seats were about level with the cab of the lorry, which is narrower than the body. It would be just possible for someone to fall out. I'm going to fight my way through the hedge and walk back along the field.'

When he returned he spoke briefly to the teacher and then came over to Fiona. 'I've found her. She's lying under the cab and I'm afraid there's a great deal of bleeding, which means medical attention is urgently needed. I think I can just squeeze underneath—it's lucky these big vehicles are high off the road—but I shall need help from someone smaller and more agile in a confined space. You!'

Fiona felt sick, but she scarcely hesitated. When he had taken what he required from the emergency bag, she followed him along the edge of a growing crop until they reached the front end of the lorry. Down on her hands and knees, she stared in horror at the mangled arm illuminated by Max's torch, and fully understood the need for her help. Somehow they had to stop the bleeding, but it was going to be very difficult in such a situation.

As they worked together trying to strap a thick pad into place, she heard in the distance the sound of a siren. The ambulances had been a long time coming, but she remembered from her stint in the accident unit that Saturday nights were the busiest of the whole week. The noise came nearer and the whole scene was brilliantly lit up so that the torch was no longer required.

'I must go and put them in the picture.' Max began to worm his way backwards. 'You stay with the child in case she comes round.'

It seemed an age before two men arrived with a stretcher, and moving the little girl was a delicate operation which could not be hurried. But at last Fiona was released from her ordeal and was able to snatch a moment of solitude in which to try and control the trembling of her legs.

'Where did you get to?' Max looked at her curiously when she reappeared. 'Feeling OK, aren't you?'

'Yes, of course.'

Two more ambulances arrived and, with well-trained speed, all the casualties were loaded in and whisked away to hospital. The bus driver went with them and soon there was no one left but the police, who were still taking notes, and the unscathed lorry driver, who was inclined to be truculent.

'Time for us to go.' Max pulled off his yellow tabard

and then looked at his watch. 'Too late for you to come back to Cornerways, so I'd better drive you home.'

'My clothes——' Fiona glanced down at Rachel's jeans and was not surprised to find that they now looked a great deal worse than when she had started out.

'I'll bring them to the surgery on Monday.' He put the emergency bag into the boot of his car and locked it. 'Are you hungry?'

'*Hungry*?' she gasped.

'No need to sound so shocked. I've been working hard since that somewhat light meal we had hours ago, and I'm starving.'

Fiona thought rapidly. Should she offer to cook him an omelette? Liz had gone off to Easterwood again and had announced her intention of staying the night whether her mother agreed or not, since her arthritis was now so bad she really needed help.

'Can't reflexology do anything for her?' Fiona had not been able to resist asking.

Liz had laughed. 'She won't even let me try! She's as rigid in her outlook as Max Whitmore, and with more excuse, seeing as she's an older generation.'

And so she had driven off that afternoon, and there was no reason for Fiona to fear awkwardness if she invited Max to supper.

'I'm rather good at omelettes,' she said casually. 'Would you care for one?'

There was a second's pause, as though she had surprised him, and then he accepted with enthusiasm.

'Ham or mushroom?' he asked as they got into the car.

'I think I could manage both.'

'Super girl!' He kissed her lightly on the cheek nearest to him, sending her pulses racing.

At Apple Acre he followed her to the kitchen and stood watching her preparations. Finding, to her astonishment, that her nausea had vanished, Fiona cooked one for herself and they sat companionably at the table and ate, finishing up with fruit and coffee.

'Can you sleep after an experience like this evening?' Max asked abruptly when they had washed up.

'I haven't had much to do with accidents, not on the spot, I mean, but I certainly don't feel sleepy at the moment.' Fiona dried her hands and hung up the towel.

'I never can. The whole damn scene goes through and through my head like a film unwinding.' He looked at her thoughtfully. 'Since you're not sleepy either, couldn't I stay a bit longer?'

Her pulse-rate had quickened again and she could not think how to answer him. Two facts stood out in her mind and wouldn't be ignored. Max attracted her physically in a way that no man had since Chris, and they were alone in the house.

'Would—would you like to listen to some music?' she asked breathlessly, answering his question indirectly.

'Music?' He sounded surprised and rather amused. 'It depends on what sort.'

'Light classical and some modern.'

He laughed. 'Are you inviting me to a concert?'

'In a way. I sometimes play my favourite tapes when I think I shan't be able to sleep, like now. Would you like to join me?'

'Sounds pleasant,' he drawled, 'but I'd like to postpone it for a few minutes.'

It was just like last time. He reached out for her with supreme self-confidence and she was powerless to resist him. She even stretched up and put both hands behind his head to draw him still closer. Just as before, her body responded to his masculinity, and a wild, passionate longing took possession of her.

They broke away at last and Max said hoarsely, 'I think we'd better start listening to that music.'

Fiona could hardly have agreed more, though she did not say so. She fetched her cassette player and a supply of tapes, and in the warm glow of two shaded lamps they settled down in armchairs at a safe distance.

At first her mind was so busy she found it impossible to concentrate on the music. To take her thoughts off what had just happened, she deliberately dwelt on the coach crash, feeling sadness and pity because of the children's unhappy end to their holiday, and the shock which their parents must by now have suffered. Gradually her taut nerves ceased twanging like guitar strings and she felt her limbs slowly relaxing into the comfortable chair.

Opposite her, Max was leaning back against the cushion with his eyes closed. 'This is nice,' he murmured sleepily. 'Very nice indeed.'

Perhaps he didn't get much home comfort in that starkly perfect house? Rachel's talents obviously lay more with interior decorating than with making a good home life for a man. Perhaps that was why her marriage had gone on the rocks?

Fiona allowed her eyelids to droop and soon she was dozing lightly, though she could still hear the music. After quite a long time she peeped at her watch and discovered it was one o'clock.

Max had evidently decided he was in bed. He had turned slightly to one side and was cradling his cheek on his hand. His hair shone reddish in the lamplight and the firm lines of his mouth had softened in sleep. He breathed regularly and deeply and did not stir when Fiona called his name quietly.

There were only two alternatives—to waken him brutally and turn him out, or to go to bed herself and let him sleep on. Rapidly making up her mind, Fiona found a scrap of paper and wrote on it, 'Gone to bed. Please don't make a noise when you leave.'

That surely couldn't be interpreted as an invitation to join her!

Upstairs she lay awake for a while, very much aware of the sleeping man downstairs, but eventually she slipped into deep unconsciousness and so heard nothing of his departure, not even the sound of his car starting up outside.

Downstairs on Sunday morning, the only thing that remained to remind her of his visit was the dent in the cushion where his head had rested.

Using quite unnecessary force, Fiona plumped it up again, and wished she could dismiss the incident from her mind as easily.

CHAPTER SIX

ON MONDAY morning Max went straight to Fiona's room when he reached the surgery and dumped a Sainsbury's carrier-bag on her desk.

'Your dress,' he said briefly.

'Thanks.' Her lips twitched. 'I hope nobody overheard you say that—they might get the wrong idea.'

'Then they'd be wasting their time.' He grinned down at her and added softly, 'More's the pity.'

She laughed and felt herself colouring. To take his attention off her slight embarrassment, she asked if he had any news of the children.

'They're doing all right except the child we rescued from under the cab. There's just a possibility they may not be able to save her arm.'

'Oh, dear, that's awful!'

'I said it's only a possibility, so there's no need to start looking on the black side just yet. The neurosurgeon at Easterwood is an extremely good bloke and if anybody can save it he will.'

'I do hope so!' she exclaimed, but he had gone.

Alone, Fiona put both the accident and what had followed it out of her mind and concentrated on work. It was a busy morning, as Monday always was, but the surgery quietened down eventually and she was beginning to think about going to lunch when she had another visitor.

Mrs McBride had waited until the patients had all

been dealt with before coming over from the house. She was a comfortable-looking woman, neatly dressed in a grey pleated skirt and blue cotton jumper. Her silver-streaked brown hair was set in rigid waves and her only make-up was a modest application of lipstick.

'Can you spare a minute, Nurse?' She stood in the doorway, smiling and looking much more sure of her welcome than the question suggested.

'Yes, of course.' Fiona jumped up and pulled forward a chair. She had met Mrs McBride several times, but only briefly on each occasion, and she felt she would like to get to know her better. Anne Marshall, that mine of information, had told her the senior doctor's wife was very well liked in the village.

'Mother's Union, WI, Flower Club—you name it, Mrs McBride belongs to it,' Anne had said. 'My mum's nearly as bad. Is yours like that?'

'Not in London!' Fiona's smile had been a little forced. 'Anyway, she's a businesswoman and wouldn't have time to join things even if she wanted to.'

She didn't have time for her daughter either, but Fiona had not mentioned that. Perhaps if she had entered the business world instead of becoming a nurse, they might have got on better. Mrs Shelton had never had much use for people whose aim in life was giving rather than getting.

This morning, as Mrs McBride sat down, Fiona reflected that the doctor and his wife must find their daughter Maggie eminently satisfactory, apart from her total lack of dress sense, and probably neither of them regarded that as important.

'What can I do for you?' she asked with a smile.

'Something which I hope will give us all pleasure.'

Jenny McBride returned the smile. 'I would like to get to know you better, and both my husband and I would be pleased if you would come to supper next Sunday evening. It's Maggie's free weekend, so she should be there, and I'm also asking poor David Kennedy. He's looked so dreadfully forlorn since his wife died and a little social life might cheer him up. I know his mother-in-law is a very nice woman, but it's *young* people he needs.' She paused to take breath and then added, 'I do hope you're free?'

'Yes, thank you,' Fiona said promptly, 'and I shall look forward to it.'

'That's settled, then.' She got up rather ponderously and pulled down her jumper. At the door she paused. 'Er—there's just one small matter I want to mention, dear. It's a little bit of gossip which came to Maggie's ears when she was on her round. She asked me if I'd give you a gentle warning.'

'Warning?' Fiona stiffened with a slight feeling of apprehension, but her conscience was clear and she was not seriously concerned.

'In a village one can't be too careful, though, of course, even in Tarling people are much more broad-minded than they used to be—not that I think that's always a good thing.'

'I'm sorry,' Fiona said helplessly, 'but I honestly haven't a clue what you're on about.'

Mrs McBride lowered her voice. 'It's just that Maggie has a patient in that terrace of cottages in Glebe Lane, near Liz Crane's house. This Mrs Jackson couldn't sleep last Saturday night and she happened to hear a car start up—well, actually it was Sunday morning, because it was three o'clock. The light from her bedroom window showed her Max Whitmore driving past. Of course Maggie said at once that he must have been out on a night call, but the woman insisted he'd come from Apple Acre and she happened to know Miss Crane was away staying with her mother, and—well—you know what I mean.'

Fiona gazed at her in blank amazement. It was all perfectly true, but what did it matter? Doing her best to hide her annoyance, she explained exactly what had happened.

Mrs McBride looked slightly uncomfortable. 'Well, of course, Maggie guessed there must be some quite innocent reason for——'

'Innocent?' Some of the anger Fiona was trying to keep battened down escaped into her voice. 'Are you suggesting that if Max and I had gone to bed together it would have been *wicked*? I don't happen to care for one-night stands, but I do believe they're a matter for the two people concerned and nothing whatsoever to do with anybody else—provided they're both free of other obligations, of course,' she added hastily.

Mrs McBride had been looking increasingly horrified at such plain speaking. 'I'm glad you included that last bit,' she said stiffly. 'You're entitled to your opinion, of course, but I would advise you to keep it to yourself while you're in Tarling. The nurse is supposed to be above reproach, and older people in the country don't understand this permissive modern outlook.' She sighed and then finished more naturally, 'I'm not at all sure I can cope with it myself—it's so different from the way my generation was brought up.'

'I'm sorry, I shouldn't have let off like that.'

'Never mind, dear, we'll say no more about it, but

do try not to get yourself into that sort of situation in future. Gossip starts so easily and is very difficult to stop.'

'I'll be more careful than I seem to have been so far,' Fiona promised.

Left alone, she sat brooding over the conversation. Perhaps she should have realised what people might think, but it had never occurred to her, used as she was to the live-and-let-live attitude of Londoners. It all seemed very petty, and she felt sure Max would agree with her. He would certainly find her immoral reputation extremely amusing!

After lunch she walked along to the supermarket to buy some tights, and as she returned she saw him driving away from a nearby house. Had he also received a warning? she wondered. The senior partner's wife would hardly take it upon herself to administer one, but perhaps Maggie might have dropped a hint. They seemed to know each other very well.

Fiona had no opportunity during the week to put out a feeler on the subject, for it was impossible to hold a private conversation with Max. He was extremely busy with a sudden outbreak of early summer flu among the schoolchildren.

But on Friday evening they chanced to meet briefly at the end of the surgery hour.

'I believe we're meeting at supper on Sunday,' Max said casually.

'Are we?' Fiona's heart had given a lurch, but her tone suggested a couldn't-care-less attitude. 'I suppose you mean at the McBrides'? I thought David Kennedy was the only man invited.'

'It seems that Maggie objected to having to share him with you and told her mother she should invite another male. Hence my last-minute invitation.'

'I see.'

When he had gone, she sat thinking for a moment before leaving, not at all sure that she did see. Maggie had never seemed to her the kind of girl who would bother too much about even numbers at the dining table, but, on the other hand, David would certainly not be equal to conducting a lively conversation with one girl, let alone two, which acounted quite plausibly for Max's invitation.

Or had Maggie asked her mother to provide not merely 'another male' but one specific man? In other words, Max Whitmore? Fiona had no answer to her puzzle, but she thought she might find one at the supper party.

On Sunday, she spent some time trying to decide what to wear. Last time she had gone out to supper she had dressed too smartly; this time she would have to get it right. But as she looked through her wardrobe an impulse came upon her to wear something outrageous—if she could find anything that warranted that description—and make them all think there might be some truth in the suspicion voiced by Maggie's patient.

Common sense prevailed and she went downstairs in a plain dark blue dress with long sleeves. Worn with important chunky jewellery it would have looked good, but Fiona had chosen gold earrings of moderate size and a simple gold chain.

'Very nice, dear,' said Liz, looking up from her desk where she was struggling with accounts. 'A bit understated, perhaps, but——'

'That's how it's meant to look.'

Fiona had already given her landlady a brief account of the previous Saturday evening—it had seemed only fair in view of the rumour apparently going round. Liz had received it with a shrug and dismissed it as unimportant.

'You'd better watch your step, though,' she had warned. 'Ninety per cent of the people in Tarling probably couldn't care less what you get up to in your spare time, but there are a few old biddies who don't have enough to do, and they're the ones you've got to look out for.' Seeing Fiona's expression, she had added hastily, 'That is, if you think their opinion matters.'

'I don't, actually. It's only because of the job I've decided to walk warily. It shouldn't be difficult. After all, Max Whitmore isn't likely to fall asleep here on another occasion, and I don't think David Kennedy is much of a menace to my reputation!'

Liz had looked at her shrewdly. 'As I said before, you've certainly been revising your opinion of Max!'

'I had to, didn't I?' Fiona had said airily. 'Nobody could be as awful as I thought he was the first time we met. But I still think he's much too bossy!'

It was a fine warm evening and she walked to the doctor's house, enjoying the quiet, almost deserted streets. The pubs had hardly started business and the fish and chip shop was closed on Sunday; there was a light in the church and the sound of singing, but only three cars parked outside.

They were all in the drawing-room when she was ushered in, except for Max, who had not yet arrived.

'My dear, how nice you look.' Jenny McBride took her hand in a warm clasp and beamed at her.

So she *had* got it right! Fiona returned the smile with enthusiasm and reflected that Mrs McBride looked very nice herself in a dress of some silky material in a warm cherry-red. Maggie, on the other hand, had as usual got it all wrong. She had avoided the clashing colours she often favoured and was wearing a surprisingly sophisticated black linen dress which was a little too tight for her generous curves. Unfortunately black did not suit her, her make-up was badly done, and her straggling dark hair managed to look untidy rather than casual.

Fiona sat down next to David, who had obviously made a great effort and looked presentable in a dark suit, though his hair needed cutting. He greeted her pleasantly and, after a small amount of verbal manoeuvring, began to talk about his collection of cactus plants.

'They were my wife's originally,' he explained, 'but after she was gone I thought it was a pity to let them die after she'd taken so much trouble with them, and then I got interested myself.'

He went on talking, rattling off a lot of Latin names, and Fiona listened and tried to make intelligent replies. Cacti had always appeared to her to consist of prickles and very little else, but it seemed that David's frequently produced flowers, which gave him great satisfaction. Under the infuence of his second sherry he confided shyly that he felt close to Mary when he was working with her precious plants.

Fiona was touched and found herself saying she would like to see the collection one day, but she did not hear his reply because Max arrived at that moment, causing a slight stir. He refused a drink, saying he was worried about a patient and might have to go out again later. As they transferred to the dining-room, Fiona found herself beside him.

'Why are you looking like a nurse tonight?' he asked, his brows raised slightly as he surveyed her unexciting appearance.

She was stung by his criticism. 'Because I *am* a nurse, I suppose,' she flung back at him.

'Rot. You were a nurse last weekend, but you didn't look like one. I much preferred the gear you had on then.'

'Too bad you don't like what I'm wearing now,' she told him in a sweet-and-sour voice. 'Mrs McBride congratulated me on it.'

'Well, she would, wouldn't she?' he murmured.

What was that supposed to mean? Fiona had no opportunity to ask him.

At the table she sat on her host's right, with David next to her and Maggie opposite with Max on her left, an arrangement which gave Fiona plenty of opportunity to observe the doctor's daughter. Before they had finished the avocado starter she had begun to suspect what she later decided was definitely the case: Maggie was head over heels in love with Max Whitmore.

She gave herself away over and over again, leaning forward to gaze into his face as she listened to what he was saying, accidentally touching his hand as she passed him the salt, looking flushed and excited and talking in a brittle kind of way quite foreign to her.

Poor girl, Fiona thought compassionately, then brought herself up with a jerk. Why *poor*? She had no reason to jump to the conclusion that Max was unlikely to return Maggie's interest in him. He might not have

quite got around to it yet, but he must be aware that
marriage between them would be a most suitable
arrangement, greatly to the advantage of both parties.
In spite of being the newest member of the practice, he
would have an assured future and would certainly step
into the position of senior partner when Dr McBride
retired.

As she thought about it, Fiona struggled to take an
objective view. She liked everything about Maggie
except her dress sense, and perhaps even that would
improve with time. A tactful husband might be able to
lead her gently towards the choice of more suitable
clothing.

She was just trying to decide whether Max could
possibly be described as tactful when she realised that
David had just finished a long rigmarole about his
hobby and was waiting for her to make some comment.
Hastily she assured him that it had been extremely
interesting and she had had no idea there was so much
to learn about the prickly objects of his devotion.

'I do hope David isn't boring you with his fixation,
dear,' Mrs McBride said later when Fiona was helping
her to carry the coffee-cups to the kitchen. 'I'm afraid
he does seem to have rather a one-track mind on social
occasions, and of course it's natural that Max should
like talking to my daughter. Did you know they were
friends at medical school? That's one reason why Max
applied for the partnership at Tarling.'

Fiona lifted the cups on her tray one by one and
carefully conveyed them to the draining-board. She was
learning a lot this evening, and not only about the
habits of cacti. None of the information she had gath-
ered was welcome, but she did not feel inclined to look

for the reason for this. She only knew she had not
enjoyed the party and would be glad when it was time
to go home.

There was the usual doubt in her mind as to when
this time could be said to have arrived. For some
reason men never seemed to be troubled with the
problem, leaving it all to their wives or girlfriends, and
as she was the only female guest she felt it was up to
her to make the first move. Accordingly she waited
until ten o'clock and then announced that she really
must go.

Max looked across at her. Maggie had monopolised
him so successfully that it was the first time he had
spoken directly to Fiona since his unfavourable comment on her appearance. 'How did you get here?' he
asked.

'I walked.'

Mrs McBride hurried to join the conversation.
'David will see you home, dear. He goes your way.'

So did Max, but at that precise moment the telephone rang, and the conversation ceased while Dr
McBride went off to answer it.

'It's for you, Max,' he called from the hall. 'That
patient you were worried about.'

A moment later Max put his head in at the door.
'Afraid I'll have to be on my way. Thanks for a super
meal, Mrs McBride,' and without a special glance at
anyone in particular he vanished.

Fiona stole a look at Maggie from beneath her lashes
and found her torn between relief and disappointment.
She must, like Fiona herself, have felt that Max had
been on the brink of offering to escort the nurse home,
and she would be glad he had been frustrated. On the

other hand, Maggie would be sorry he had had to dash off in such a hurry instead of saying goodnight properly.

Fiona went off with David wondering what was in store for her and determined to fend off anything even remotely affectionate. She need not have worried. Her escort talked all the way about his wife and her tragic death after only four years of marriage. But just before they reached Apple Acre he changed the subject.

'I didn't think the old man looked at all well,' he said.

'Dr McBride?' Fiona had been so busy observing his daughter with Max that she had not given her host much close attention. Certainly he had been rather quiet, but she did not know him very well and this had not surprised her. 'You've known him a lot longer than I have,' she hedged. 'What did you notice particularly?'

'I thought he looked a bit drawn.'

People usually looked drawn when they were in pain. 'Perhaps he had indigestion?' Fiona suggested.

'Could be, I suppose.'

They had reached the gate and halted, peering at each other uncertainly in the darkness, for there were no street lamps in Glebe Lane.

'Where do you live?' she asked hurriedly, to break the silence.

'Only another five minutes' walk from here. I like to leave the car at home when I haven't got far to go. . .' His voice died away uncertainly.

All Fiona's instincts were telling her he was about to kiss her, though she didn't think he really wanted to. She made a move to escape before he could get around to it, but found she had left it too late. David suddenly put his arm round her shoulders, planted a hurried kiss on her cheek and departed with a muttered farewell.

She stood looking after him for a moment, dismayed to find her eyes full of tears. She had absolutely nothing to cry about, she told herself as she walked up the path. The incident had been silly and unnecessary, but certainly not in the least upsetting. So why did she feel unhappy?

Refusing to answer the question, Fiona blinked rapidly and went into the house. She found Liz just going to bed and gave her an animated account of the evening, including Maggie's too obvious interest in Max, though she dealt with it in as kindly a way as possible and did not mention her dress.

'That girl's never had a proper boyfriend,' Liz said. 'I've known her since she was at school and always liked her, though there were times when I could have shaken her. I believe she's quite a good doctor, particularly when dealing with children, but in personal relationships she's so naïve it just isn't true—except in her case it's only too true,' she added incoherently.

'I never met anybody like her before.'

'I'm not surprised. It would have done Maggie good to spend at least a couple of years at London hospitals. Instead of that, as soon as she qualified she worked as a house physician at Easterwood for the shortest possible time and then joined the practice.'

'Is she an only child?'

'Oh, no.' Liz made sure the front door was bolted. 'She's got two older brothers, neither of them doctors. They're both married and live their own lives.'

'I expect that's made Maggie kind of extra special to

her parents,' Fiona said thoughtfully. 'The only girl and the only one to follow in father's footsteps. You can see they both adore her.'

Undressing, she put Maggie McBride out of her mind, along with David Kennedy and Max Whitmore. She had a great deal of trouble with Max, who tended to invade her thoughts every time she relaxed her grip on them, but eventually she succeeded and sleep claimed her.

In the morning she was glad to start work again. Next weekend, she decided, she would if possible avoid invitations to supper and spend a carefree time exploring the neighbourhood—by herself.

The week was uneventful, and when Saturday came everything went according to plan, except that Fiona had not anticipated a slight feeling of loneliness. Shrugging it off, she went for several walks, including a long one on Sunday afternoon. This brought her back to Tarling by a footpath which came on to a road near the new houses which she had so much disliked when she'd visited Cornerways. They weren't too bad, she decided now, and some of them had beautiful gardens.

A bright spot of colour caught her eye and she saw a little girl of about two wearing a miniature scarlet tracksuit. She was leaning over a small pool, poking something with a stick and totally absorbed. Fiona had just time to hope the water wasn't very deep when a car stopped and the driver asked for directions to Easterwood.

She had done hardly any driving in the neighbourhood since her arrival and childhood memories were useless, so she had to do some quick thinking before she could give adequate instructions. When she glanced back at the pretty scene, the little figure had vanished.

Fiona never knew what made her hesitate before walking on. The child had almost certainly run into the house, perhaps called by her mother. Nevertheless, she felt vaguely uneasy. It wouldn't take a minute to open the gate and invade the garden, just to satisfy herself the child had *not* fallen into the pool.

A moment later she knew she had been right to listen to that inner voice of warning.

Weighed down by her waterlogged tracksuit and tangled up in lilies and other aquatic plants, the child was lying face down and motionless. She must have fallen in just as the car stopped. How long ago was that? Fiona didn't dare even to guess, she was far too busy. Down on her knees, she grabbed the wet clothing and heaved. The little girl was astonishingly heavy in her sodden condition, but somehow she hauled her out and laid her flat. With a sick feeling of horror she realised that breathing had stopped.

Was the heart still beating? Having established that it was, Fiona started mouth-to-mouth resuscitation, squeezing the tiny nostrils and remembering to breathe very gently into the open mouth. Vaguely she was aware that a girl had run from the house and was kneeling beside her, babbling frantic questions, but she ignored her and kept steadily on.

Someone else joined them, a young man—presumably the father—and soon after that a car drew up at the gate. A voice from behind said urgently, 'Shall I take over?'

Max's voice?

But she didn't need any help. The child had drawn a

natural, quivering breath, and very carefully Fiona
turned her over into the recovery position and smiled
triumphantly at the young parents.

'She'll be OK now,' she said confidently.

There were a few minutes of hysterical thanks,
confused conversation and a solemn warning from
Max.

'You'd better put a net over that pool if you don't
want a repetition of this. There might not happen to be
a nurse passing next time.'

Followed by fervent promises and renewed thanks,
they walked away together. 'You did a good job there,'
he added warmly to Fiona as they reached the road.

'It was lucky I was handy. How did you get to know
about it?'

'The father phoned me and I leapt into the car and
came round. It was no distance.' He paused with a
hand on the car door. 'Can I give you a lift?'

'No, thanks. I'll finish my walk.' Fiona gave him a
bright, impersonal smile and tramped on.

Max stared after her, frowning. If she wanted to be
like that, then he was quite willing to let her get on
with it, or so he told himself.

Fiona gave Liz a dramatic account of her adventure
and they spent the evening watching television. In the
morning the surgery was, as usual after a weekend,
very busy and Fiona did not get her mid-morning coffee
until nearly lunchtime. She was relaxing with it in her
room when Anne rang through on the intercom to say
someone wanted to see her.

'The name's Rachel Blackmore,' she added.

For a moment it meant nothing, and then Fiona
realised it might be Max's sister, whose surname she

had never heard. 'You'd better tell her to come in,' she said reluctantly.

She was right in her guess and she tried to make her visitor welcome, offering a chair and coffee, and commenting on the weather, but Rachel refused the coffee and ignored the small talk.

'I've come about reflexology,' she announced. 'I've hurt my shoulder and I believe that woman you live with can put it right.'

CHAPTER SEVEN

'REFLEXOLOGY!' Fiona did not attempt to hide her surprise.

'That's what I said,' Rachel confirmed impatiently. 'I strained my shoulder heaving the rotary mower about in the orchard and it's keeping me awake at night— just as I was beginning to sleep better too,' she added ruefully.

'Have you seen a doctor?'

'Max poked at it and said it would clear up in time, but he wasn't a bit sympathetic. In fact, he as good as said it was all my own fault. I told him he'd got a nerve because if he was sensible and employed somebody to do the rough work I wouldn't have to cut the grass. We had a bit of a row about it and I said he was the most stupidly stubborn man I'd ever met, not excepting my husband.'

'What did he say to that?' Fiona asked with interest.

Rachel smiled fleetingly. 'He lost his temper.' She looked straight at Fiona. 'I'm still waiting for you to tell me about this reflexology thing.'

Fiona hesitated and then said cautiously, 'Why don't you ask Miss Crane?'

'Because she'd be prejudiced, and there does seem to be a lot of controversy about the treatment. I thought I might get a balanced view from you.'

'I'm afraid you're not going to get any view at all, because I've no personal knowledge of it. I've been told about people who've benefited tremendously, but that's all hearsay, and you must know your own brother is dead against it.'

'Of course I know, and that's partly why I want to consult Miss Crane. It would make Max hopping mad.'

Fiona suppressed a smile. 'Not the best of reasons,' she pointed out gently.

'I don't care!' Rachel stood up, but made no move towards the door. 'I'm disappointed in you. I thought you'd at least tell me what the treatment consists of. I like to know what I'm letting myself in for.'

There seemed to be no harm in that, and Fiona gave her visitor a brief description of the way Liz manipulated her patients' feet.

'Sounds crazy!' Rachel commented. 'But I think I'll give it a go, just for the hell of it if nothing else. Could you make an appointment for me?'

'It would be much better if you ring up and do it yourself, but I'll give you the number.' She tore off a sheet from her memo pad and scribbled it down.

'Thanks a lot.' Rachel put it in her bag and opened the door. 'I knew it would be a good idea to talk to you. I was dithering before I came, but now I've quite made up my mind to see the reflexologist. I'm very grateful to you for your advice.' With a nonchalant wave of her hand she left the room.

Had she given any advice? Fiona wondered when Rachel had gone. She certainly hadn't meant to, for she knew she should not recommend alternative medicine while actually working in a general practice. Thinking over the conversation she decided her conscience was completely clear. She had made no attempt to encourage Rachel to consult Liz, and surely it wasn't a crime to give her the phone number?

Satisfied, she poured away the remains of her cold coffee and went to make some more.

That evening Liz said suddenly, 'Guess who rang me up today!'

'Rachel Blackmore,' Fiona said promptly.

'How on earth did you know?' When the explanation had been given, the reflexologist said thoughtfully, 'She didn't mention her brother's opinion of my profession and I think it would be fair to say she was without prejudice. I certainly hope I shall be able to do something for her, and I've booked her in to start treatment next Wednesday.'

It was the first time Fiona had actually known any of Liz's patients and she looked forward to being told eventually whether the treatment had been successful. When Wednesday came she remembered the appointment and found time to speculate whether Rachel had told her brother about it.

On Thursday morning she hadn't been in her office long before she found an answer to that particular question.

'I'd like a word with you, Nurse.'

Fiona had her head in the cupboard, checking sterile dressings, and had not heard anyone enter the room. She swung round hastily at the sound of Max's voice and faced him with a slight quiver of apprehension. His expression told her at once that he was not in a good mood.

'What can I do for you?' she asked quietly, moving across to her desk and standing very erect on the other side of it.

'You can explain what you mean by daring to give unorthodox medical advice to my sister.' He glowered at her, his blue eyes dangerously bright.

Fiona drew herself up even straighter and gave her indignation full rein. 'I most strongly deny that I gave Rachel any advice. She was already interested in reflexology when she came to see me, and all I did was to tell her to ask Liz Crane about it.'

'That woman.'

Fiona's lips tightened. She struggled for a moment to control her own anger, then flung discretion to the winds. 'I do wish you wouldn't keep calling her that, Doctor! Liz is a very nice person and absolutely sincere in her work. You're perfectly entitled to disagree with it—though I can't help thinking it's rather fuddy-duddy of you—but you've no right to be rude about her behind her back.'

'I would be rude to her face if we were talking about reflexology,' he growled.

'I don't doubt it.' In spite of her annoyance, Fiona's lips twitched. 'But we're getting away from the subject we were discussing, and that—in case you've forgotten—is the advice I'm supposed to have given to your sister. I was extremely careful *not* to give her any advice, but I did give her Liz's phone number to save her the bother of looking it up. I considered that a mere courtesy.'

'Huh!' Max frowned down at the floor and shifted his ground. 'Rachel knew my views on reflexology and that's why she came here behind my back——'

'Your sister isn't a child, Dr Whitmore. She's a grown woman and can surely please herself about what she does.' Seeing from his expression that he had no answer handy, Fiona went on triumphantly, 'It would have been quite easy for her to keep quiet about the whole thing, but she's obviously told you she's going to have treatment, and I don't see you can call that going behind your back.' Restraining herself from adding a somewhat childish, 'So there!' she finished coolly, 'Was there anything else you wanted to see me about, because I'm very busy?'

Max looked startled, mumbled that there was nothing and departed, leaving the door open. Fiona looked after him with a rueful smile. He wasn't used to being dismissed like a schoolboy, and maybe it would do him good.

But she didn't think it likely.

She had a clinic that afternoon for people suffering from deafness and one of her patients was the Mrs Walsh whom she had met on her first morning, whose husband had been a gardener at Cornerways.

'You've never come to see us,' the woman said reproachfully, 'and George and me would love to have a talk about the old days.'

After seeing what Rachel had done to the house, Fiona had been trying to forget the old days. Besides, she had been accused of indulging too much in nostalgia and, deep down in her heart, she was aware of the truth of this. But the temptation was great and, besides, she would like to meet again the nice old man who had always given her the biggest rosiest apple.

'I wasn't sure if you'd want me just to drop in,' she excused herself. 'It might not be convenient.'

'We wouldn't have minded,' Mrs Walsh told her warmly, 'but it'd be even better if you came to tea. How about next Saturday?'

'Lovely! I shall look forward to it.'

It was a beautiful afternoon when she set out to walk to Bridge Cottage. While she had been busy accustoming herself to her new life, summer had been getting well established. There were French marigolds now in the windowboxes at the Fox, and several cottages had climbing roses in full flower. The one where George Walsh and his wife lived had an exotic mauve clematis reaching nearly to the roof, and the tiny front garden was immaculate with bedding plants. When Fiona walked round the house, instinctively making for the back door as was the country custom, she admired the orderly rows of flowers and vegetables in the rear garden.

The man using a hoe with rhythmic movements turned as she appeared, and she saw that he wasn't really old at all—perhaps only in his late fifties— though he had appeared so ancient in her childhood.

'Afternoon, miss,' he greeted her, just as though they had met last week. 'Lovely day.'

Fiona praised his garden and then his wife called him to come in and wash his hands, and they entered the house together. The years rolled away as they talked over the delicious tea laid out ceremoniously in the front room, and it seemed to Fiona that every other sentence started with, 'Do you remember. . .?'

They did not mention the present state of Cornerways until the meal was nearly finished.

'Have you seen it lately?' Fiona asked.

George shook his head. 'No, but you get to hear things in a village, and I know the garden's been let go something shocking. Seems a pity.'

For some reason Fiona felt compelled to defend

Max. 'Dr Whitmore is quite a keen gardener, I believe, but he just hasn't the time to look after it properly. I'm sure he does his best.'

'It doesn't make sense to me.' Mrs Walsh poured Fiona a third cup of tea. 'A young chap like that didn't ought to be spoiling his hands with garden dirt when he's a doctor and should be taking care of them.'

'I expect he finds it a relaxation.' They both looked at her uncomprehendingly and she continued hurriedly, 'But I do agree it would be better if he had professional help.' An idea flashed into her mind and she put it into words without stopping to think. 'Why don't you go along, George, and ask if you could lend a hand for a few hours a week—that is, if you've got the time? He might be grateful.'

And he might not, her more cautious self reminded her, but it was too late now.

'I dunno, I'm sure.' He scratched his grizzled head. 'Maybe the doctor'd think it an impertinence.'

'Nurse wouldn't have suggested it if she'd thought that,' his wife interposed. 'I expect she knows Dr Whitmore pretty well by now.'

There was a strange little pause and Fiona suddenly remembered the warning Mrs McBride had given her. Did this nice couple know about the shocking reputation she had so innocently acquired? If so, they clearly had no intention of mentioning it, for George had gone on to wonder audibly whether he could find the time for helping out at Cornerways.

By the time she left, it had been decided by husband and wife that the gardener should ride his bicycle over to Cornerways at some time when he thought Max might be there—probably at the weekend—and tentatively offer his services.

'And if he doesn't like the idea, he can say so and no harm done. I shan't take offence, seeing as I shall have stuck me neck right out.' George grinned, showing pipe-stained teeth.

Walking home, Fiona wished she had not made the suggestion, but it was done now and there was no point in worrying about it. Very likely she would never hear any more on the subject.

For a time no mention of it came her way, but after the following weekend Rachel appeared again. This time she was smiling.

'I just popped in to tell you about my first reflexology treatment, Fiona. It was a bit painful—in my feet, not my shoulder, that feels better already. I've got another appointment this week and Miss Crane thinks she can cure it completely. Isn't that wonderful?'

'Super!' Fiona returned the smile. 'So it was worth the row with your brother?'

Rachel stared. 'What do you know about that?'

'He accused me of influencing you.'

'He what? Oh, *really*—Max is just about the limit! I hope you told him he'd got it all wrong.'

'Er—yes, I certainly did. He wasn't very pleased.'

'Don't let that worry you.' Rachel turned to leave, but paused in the doorway. 'By the way, I've done another awful thing, but Max doesn't know yet. On Sunday, when he'd been called out to an accident, an old chap turned up on an ancient bicycle and offered to help in the garden a couple of hours a week. I engaged him on the spot. See you!'

Fiona looked after her in dismay, shrugged and dismissed the matter from her mind.

That week Max had an unexpected summons from a patient on holiday at the seaside about twenty miles away. He could have suggested the woman called in a local doctor, but twenty miles was nothing really and he fancied a breath of sea air. Rachel might enjoy it too, he reflected, and rang up to announce that he would take her with him.

'Oh—well, I don't know——' she began uncertainly.

'You've got nothing else to do, have you?'

'N-no, but——'

'Then I'll be along in five minutes. Mind you're ready.' Without waiting for any further protest, he rang off.

She was upstairs when he reached Cornerways and called down to say she was changing into a dress. Since she had taken rather more interest in her appearance lately and he regarded that as a good sign, Max merely told her to hurry up and wandered out into the garden.

He was amazed to discover a bicycle leaning against one of the outhouses, and further away down the garden a man was weeding the border.

Max reached him in a few long strides. 'Who the devil are you?' he demanded.

Very slowly the man straightened his back and stood with his hands on his hips. He was nearly as tall as Max and there was an air of dignity about him. 'My name's George Walsh,' he said quietly. 'The young lady thought you needed a bit of help in the garden.'

'She did, did she? How long have you been working here without my knowing?'

'This is the first time, sir. As for you not knowing, that's no concern of mine. It was the lady as engaged me, like I said.' George cast a disparaging eye at the summer growth of weeds which Max had found it impossible to cope with. 'I used to work here in the old days and it'd be a real pleasure to do what I can towards making the garden a bit more shipshape. That's if you don't raise no objection.'

For a moment Max was too taken aback to speak, and then he muttered, 'Carry on,' and stalked back towards the yard, a terrible suspicion nagging at his mind.

Was it possible that Fiona, with her fixation on Cornerways, had engaged this fellow to work in the garden? Surely even she would not do such a thing, and yet. . .

Rachel was coming down the stairs, wearing a cream summer dress patterned with leaves, and she eyed him warily. But before she could say anything Max burst into speech.

'Why wasn't I told about that gardener chap?'

'It's only been fixed up a day or two. I just never got around to it, that's all. It doesn't matter, does it?'

'So you *did* know about it?'

She stared at him. 'Of course I knew, Max. Are you out of your mind? I engaged the man—didn't he tell you?'

'He said a young lady had asked him to work here for a couple of hours weekly, and just for a moment I wondered if Fiona—well, you know what she's like about this place.'

'She'd never do that! It would be colossal cheek and not like her at all, but I think she had a hand in it, all the same. This man Walsh knew her when she used to stay here as a child and, though he didn't actually say so, he hinted that she'd said something about your needing a gardener, and that's why he called.'

Max's indignation was out of all proportion to the importance of the incident, and he was uneasily aware of it. He stood frowning in the hall, lost in thought, and only Rachel's voice recalled him to the present.

'I thought you said you were in a hurry. I changed at terrific speed, and now you're keeping me waiting.'

'No, I'm not. We had to sort out this gardener business.'

'We could have done that as we went along,' she pointed out, snatching the last word.

He let her have it, pleased that she was showing more animation, and stored the matter away at the back of his mind. They drove amicably to the sea and would have liked to linger there, but Max had other calls to make and they returned at speed. He dropped his sister at the corner near the house and then made for East Lane. If he was lucky, he might catch Fiona before she went home.

He was luckier even than that. As he turned into the lane he saw her tall, slender figure coming towards him, and rejoiced that they could have their conversation away from the surgery.

'Get in,' he ordered, leaning across and opening the door for her.

She looked at him in surprise, making no move to obey. 'Why?' she asked flatly.

Max resisted the temptation to state equally flatly, 'Because I say so,' and announced that he wanted to talk to her and could spare a few minutes for the purpose.

'About a patient?'

'No.' And seeing her still hesitating, he added brusquely, 'About George Walsh.'

'Oh!' There was a sudden wariness in her eyes. 'Do we have to?'

'Yes, I'm afraid we do. For goodness' sake, *get in*!'

Rather to his surprise, Fiona abandoned her resistance and slipped into the car. But as Max drove back to the High Street, she made one more protest.

'I really can't see there's anything to talk about.'

'In that case, we must agree to differ—as usual.' He slowed down for the narrow bridge and then speeded up as they left Tarling behind.

'Where on earth are we going?' Fiona demanded.

'Only to the Heath. It's no distance, and we can talk there without the whole village knowing.'

They did not speak again until he swung the car off the road and along a rough sandy track leading to a picnic site. Earlier it had been full of people exercising dogs or just strolling in the sunshine, but at present it was deserted. Max halted facing a vast expanse of heather, not yet in bloom, and for a brief moment they sat watching some rabbits who had fled at their approach but quickly returned to nibble.

For some reason Fiona's heart was beating painfully fast. Afraid that he might notice her uneven breathing, she was the first to speak. 'I wish you'd tell me why you've kidnapped me and brought me here. Liz will be wondering where I am.'

'Rubbish. She'll take it for granted that something

has cropped up at the surgery.' Max slid his arm along the back of her seat, further increasing her tension.

'Why do you want to talk about George?' she persisted. 'I can't see there's anything to say.'

'There's this. You've been interfering again, haven't you? You didn't like the state of my garden, so you suggested to the previous gardener that he might put in a few hours getting it into the kind of order *you* thought was right for it.' He took a deep breath and went surging on. 'It was a stroke of luck for you that when he came Rachel was there alone, and I expect he saw at a glance she was a soft touch and——'

Fiona was so angry she whirled round in her seat and pushed his arm violently from the back of it. 'How *dare* you say things like that? You're making me out to be the sort of loathsome person who's always sticking her nose into other people's affairs. You tried to do it when you made that stupid fuss about your sister having reflexology treatment, and now you're at it again over George Walsh. He and his wife are old friends of mine, and of course we talked about Cornerways when I went to tea with them. What else would we talk about, for goodness' sake?'

There was no need for her to admit it had been her idea that George should return to work at her grandparents' old home, and originally she had hoped Max would never find out. Now her fury ensured that she no longer cared.

'Naturally I suggested you might like a bit of help, and I was pleased when George said he would go along and see you. I never expected Rachel would be the one to take him on, but I'm glad now that she did, because you would have certainly turned him down flat.'

Max had listened in silence to her tirade, but when she had finished he calmly replaced his arm along the back of her seat and, with his other hand, took hold of her chin and turned her head towards him.

'It's quite an experience to see you lose that icy control of yours and really let fly,' he said calmly. 'One of these days I shan't be able to resist the temptation to provoke you deliberately, just to see the result.'

'Don't you ever dare——'

'Why not? It's good for you to be ruled by your emotions occasionally, even if the outburst is only caused by rage.' Max paused, and then added softly, 'If the emotion in question should happen to be something quite the opposite of rage, I should think the experience would be even more interesting.'

Fiona could think of nothing to say. She was trembling a little and trying to hide it. As Max's arm slipped from the back of the seat to her shoulders she made no protest. She was as eager for his kiss as if she had been a teenager learning about love. Her lips parted slightly, she leaned towards him in instinctive surrender, and the roughness of his cheek was more sensual than if it had been smooth and scented with aftershave.

When Max released her abruptly she fell back against the seat, her heart pounding, and with an unhappy sense of rejection. To get rid of it, she whipped up her indignation. He always calmly assumed she would be willing whenever he happened to feel in the mood to kiss her, and the really infuriating part was that he was usually right.

'I wish you wouldn't do that,' she said sharply as he started the engine.

She was half expecting him to say, 'Liar!' as he had

done once before, but instead of that he only asked calmly, 'Why not?' and added, apparently as an after-thought, 'It's very pleasant.'

Fiona ignored that and sought desperately for a valid reason for her objection. 'Because it doesn't make sense. Quite a lot of the time you're horrible to me, and——'

'Horrible?' Max exclaimed in astonishment.

'That's what I said, and I meant it too. You're always complaining about things I say and do, and then you expect me to submit to—to being kissed just because it boosts your masculine ego. I don't have any use for that sort of behaviour.'

She was expecting an explosion of wrath, but he had his eyes fixed on the road and was apparently concen-trating on getting back to Tarling as quickly as possible. When he did eventually speak his voice was so low she only just caught the words.

'I suppose it's never occurred to you that a bloke needs some form of self-defence?'

CHAPTER EIGHT

FIONA puzzled over Max's words all the way home, and afterwards too. Did he mean he needed to defend himself against *her*? And, if so, why did he feel the necessity? Eventually she shrugged and dismissed the matter from her mind. Or tried to.

During the next two weeks she saw very little of him. David Kennedy was on holiday and there was extra work for the other three doctors, and in addition the summer traffic caused a crop of accidents in the neighbourhood which took up a considerable amount of Max's time.

And then, one morning, he appeared in her room.

'Rachel says we ought to ask you to come and inspect your gardener pal's transformation,' he announced. 'I've had instructions to invite you to supper on Sunday.'

As an invitation it left a great deal to be desired, and Fiona was on the brink of pretending she had a prior engagement. Nevertheless, curiosity—was it *only* curiosity?—urged her to accept.

'How's your sister?' she asked politely.

Max looked down at her and raised his eyebrows. 'Meaning precisely what?'

For a moment she had forgotten about the reflexology treatment and had been referring to Rachel's state of mind. She had no wish to embark on yet another argument about Liz's profession, and at the same time didn't want Max to imagine she was avoiding it.

'Meaning just generally,' she told him airily.

'She's certainly much less depressed and I have great hopes she's on an even keel again. As for her shoulder, hasn't your friend Liz Crane boasted to you that she's worked another of her so-called miracles? The shoulder is almost cured and one more session should put it completely right.'

'Liz doesn't discuss her patients with me, but I'm very glad to hear she's been so successful.' Trying to conceal her jubilation, she added rashly, 'Has this made you view reflexology differently?'

'No,' he said curtly.

Fiona was so exasperated, she burst out, 'I don't see how you can say that after telling me Liz has worked a miracle.'

Unexpectedly he grinned. 'It wasn't the treatment that did Rachel so much good. It was her own belief in reflexology. It's all in the mind, just as I've always thought. See you on Sunday, and come early so you can inspect the garden before supper.'

He went out looking pleased with himself and Fiona was left fuming. Fortunately, the arrival of Mrs Forbes for her second anti-tetanus injection took her mind off the unsatisfactory conversation. 'Did you enjoy your holiday?' she asked, noting the nervous tension which was making the patient sit tautly on the edge of her chair.

'Not very much,' Janet confessed, averting her eyes from the hypodermic Fiona was preparing. 'Does that shock you? It does me. We went to Frinton, and the weather was lovely and the children played on the beach every day. If I were a proper grandmother, I would have been in my element, but half the time I was bored. I felt terribly guilty about it.'

'I don't see any reason why you should,' Fiona told her, anxious to keep the conversation going so as to take Mrs Forbes's mind off the dreaded jab. 'Just having grandchildren doesn't automaticaly make you into the conventional grandmother. Why should it? You're a person in your own right and you'll go on being one.'

'What a comforting girl you are!' She held out her arm almost without noticing it. 'You listened to me so sympathetically the last time I came, and now you're doing it again. You must be a wonderful nurse.'

It was impossible not to enjoy the fulsome praise, and Fiona thanked her prettily. 'Anyway,' she finished, 'the whole of Tarling thinks you're doing a wonderful job with David's children—if that's any consolation to you.'

'Of course it is. I just wish I could see an end to it, that's all.' Janet Forbes sighed. 'If only he would marry again—I know my daughter would have wanted it, provided he chose wisely, of course.'

Fiona dabbed surgical spirit on the injection site. 'Is there any hope of that?' she asked cautiously.

'There doesn't seem to be. When I first came I had high hopes of Maggie McBride. She's so nice, and genuinely fond of children, but David seems quite uninterested.'

And Maggie had her sights fixed elsewhere, Fiona reflected, but she said nothing aloud. Her silence caused the patient to glance at her curiously and it was impossible not to notice the flash of speculation in her eyes.

So this was another person who hoped she might marry David Kennedy. She couldn't blame Mrs Forbes for allowing the thought to pass through her mind, but she did wish people would leave her future alone. She had no idea herself what it might hold, and no one else had any right even to guess.

As she wrote the next appointment—in six months' time—on the small blue card, it was impossible not to wonder what the intervening months would bring. As far as she herself was concerned, one thing was clear. If Chris came back into her life she would no longer feel anything except a mild friendliness towards him. Her love for him was completely dead.

But that didn't mean she wanted to replace him with someone else. Certainly not David Kennedy.

Fiona set out on Sunday evening with mixed feelings. It was impossible not to remember the previous occasion, the school coach accident which had followed supper and the interlude at Glebe Lane after that.

As she neared Cornerways her attention was caught by a strange car which stood outside. There was no other house anywhere near, so it must have some connection with the inhabitants.

Max opened the door in answer to her ring and stared at her blankly. 'Good God! I'd completely forgotten.'

'That I was invited to supper? You certainly do have a gift for saying just the right thing.'

'No, you twit.' He grinned and momentarily lost his air of abstraction. 'I'd forgotten you were coming early.

Not that there's likely to be any supper even later on, but at least you can see the garden and tell me if you approve.'

Totally confused by the greeting, Fiona followed him through the house towards the back door. As they passed the sitting-room she could hear a murmur of voices, one definitely a man's, and as soon as they were outside in the yard Max explained what had happened.

'Rachel's husband has turned up, right out of the blue without a word of warning. It was an awful shock for her, but I must say she seemed to rally remarkably quickly. They've been talking non-stop ever since.' He stood aside to allow Fiona to precede him down the garden path.

Neither of them admired George's neat borders, or even noticed them. They were far too busy wondering what was going on in the house they had left.

'Does he want Rachel to go back to him?' Fiona asked. 'I believe you said they were separated, not divorced.'

'That's right. To my mind it would be the best thing for them both, but only if they're prepared to make concessions. Tony's an architect and Rachel, as you know, is an interior decorator. They both need to stop concentrating so hard on their professions and give a little more time to each other. Then I reckon they'd be OK.'

'Do you think they'll be able to see that for themselves?' Fiona halted beside a clump of delphiniums which, though she was unaware of it, complemented the soft blue of her dress.

Although Max answered her with a fervent, 'I certainly hope so,' his eyes were on the picture she made with her background of flowers and her blonde hair hanging free. 'Is the garden to your liking?' he asked abruptly.

'I haven't looked at it,' she admitted with a laugh.

Together they briefly inspected George's handiwork, though neither of them gave it the attention it deserved. When they reached the small orchard, they stopped and began slowly to retrace their steps.

'I hoped the strawberries would be ripe,' Max said, 'but it doesn't matter now, since we shan't be here for supper.'

'I expect you'd like me to quietly disappear,' Fiona suggested.

He stared at her in astonishment. 'I most certainly would not! Whatever gave you that idea?'

'It's obvious, surely? I was invited to supper, and as there apparently isn't going to be any——'

'We have to eat. I'll take you out for a meal instead.'

'Oh!' She coloured with pleasure. 'That would be lovely.'

'It won't be a pub meal like the last time. With you looking so fetching in that dress, we can go somewhere nice. How about The Old Barn at Somerwell?'

'Anywhere you say. I don't know anything about eating-places in the neighbourhood.'

He left her in the garden and went indoors to change. When he returned he was wearing a dark green shirt with collar and tie, and light cotton trousers. His reddish hair shone with brushing and he had found time to shave.

It was ten miles to Somerwell and they did not speak much on the drive. When they parked outside The Old Barn, Fiona looked at it with interest. Outside it appeared precisely that, but inside it had been transformed into an intimate restaurant with adjoining bar. Max had rung up before they left Tarling and a table had been reserved for them in a corner half hidden by luxuriant plants. The mutually friendly mood in which they had started out continued without being marred by disagreement, and they lingered over their meal, talking on topics which interested them both.

If only it could always be like this, Fiona thought wistfully.

She had not enjoyed herself so much for a long time, and she responded to the atmosphere by allowing her personality to unfold like the petals of a flower which only opened in sunshine.

Well fed, relaxed and contented, they left The Old Barn at last and strolled hand in hand towards the car park. It was late but still not quite dark, though the stars could plainly be seen overhead and a young moon peeped at them coyly above a dark mass of Forestry Commission trees. It was a night for romance, and Fiona, though she would not have put it into words even in her own mind, knew that her mood was in accordance with it.

Max drove slowly as though he did not want the evening to end, but soon Fiona realised he was looking for something. Eventually he found it, a narrow untarmacked lane with grass verges leading nowhere as far as they could tell and quite deserted.

'It's a pity to hurry home,' he murmured, swinging the car on to the grass and switching off the engine.

'It's certainly a lovely evening,' she agreed.

He chuckled, his arms already reaching out for her. 'I didn't bring you here to talk about the weather!'

'I never supposed you did,' was all she had time to murmur before his lips silenced her.

Fiona closed her eyes and experienced again that wonderful melting sensation in all her limbs. Her mind felt empty and her whole body gloriously alive; all she wanted was to submit, to live in the present and forget both past and future.

But suddenly a harsh, discordant sound shattered the silence and flung them apart as violently as though it had been a shutter coming down from above and tearing them from each other's arms.

The car phone was ringing.

Max muttered something and stretched his hand out to stop the noise. Please, not another accident, Fiona was saying inside her head, even though she knew her desperate pleading couldn't possibly influence what was going to happen.

It was not an accident. It was Maggie McBride in a state of barely controlled panic.

'Oh, Max, I'm so glad I've managed to get you! Something terrible's happened—it's Dad—he's had a stroke. Can you come at once? And please hurry—he's pretty bad.'

'Have you sent for an ambulance?'

'You think I should do that before you get here?'

'I certainly do, if it's as bad as you say, but I'm not far away—I may get there first.' Max replaced the phone and started the engine. 'Did you hear that?' he flung at Fiona, who had sat silent and stricken.

'Most of it. Are we going straight there?'

'Of course. You weren't expecting me to drop you off first, were you?'

'Oh, no, but I don't suppose there'll be anything I can do with two doctors on the spot.'

'You might be able to look after Mrs McBride. She's sure to be suffering from shock.'

It took only fifteen minutes to reach Tarling, and when they turned into East Lane they saw that they had beaten the ambulance.

A white-faced Maggie opened the door, and a tiny part of Fiona's mind registered the fact that she was much more attractive without her florid colouring.

'He's lying where he fell.' Maggie's voice was breathless with fear. 'It was impossible for Mother and me to move him, but we tried to make him comfortable—not that he'd be aware of it,' she added forlornly. Suddenly she saw Fiona standing quietly in the background and exclaimed, 'You've brought the nurse with you!'

The end of the sentence had risen slightly, but no one answered the implied question. It would have been difficult to do so.

'Where is he?' Max was already in the hall.

'In the dining-room. We'd been sitting talking over a late supper and Dad seemed quite all right except that he hadn't eaten much, and it happened as he got up from the table.'

The door of the dining-room was wide open and Max paused to look in. Dr McBride had knocked his chair over when he collapsed, and he now lay with his head between its legs, supported by a cushion. He was unconscious, his face an unhealthy colour beneath his beard, and breathing stertorously with his mouth dragged down on one side. His wife was on her knees beside him, her plump figure both awkward and pathetic in the unaccustomed position.

She said emotionally, 'Oh, Max, I'm so glad you've come! Maggie's too upset to give an opinion on her own father, but I must know how bad he is.'

'No, I'm not, Mother. I told you almost immediately that it was a severe seizure.'

'I agree with the diagnosis,' Max put in quietly, 'but you mustn't be too alarmed, Mrs McBride. People make wonderful recoveries from strokes these days.'

During the brief conversation Fiona had remained in the background, but she felt the need to justify her presence and now came forward. 'Do let me help you into a chair,' she said gently to Mrs McBride. 'You'll be much more comfortable while you wait.' Extending a hand, she assisted the distraught woman to her feet. 'I expect you'd like a cup of tea?'

'Thank you, dear. That would be very nice.'

The words had been spoken mechanically, and Fiona doubted whether her suggestion had penetrated very far into the fog of distress in which Mrs McBride was floundering. But she knew the hot tea would help if she could get it ready in time, and perhaps Maggie would like a cup too.

She had only just plugged in the kettle when she heard the ambulance approaching. The tea obviously wouldn't be wanted now, but she lingered in the kitchen until the bustle in the hall had ceased. She was just going to reappear when Max put his head in.

'I'm going to drive to the hospital to bring Maggie and her mother back. I suppose you can see yourself home?'

'Yes, of course. Don't worry about me.'

'There's enough to worry about without adding you

to the list,' he said grimly. 'Thank heaven David's back from holiday.'

Until then Fiona had felt only concern for the senior partner, whom she genuinely liked, but now she realised he would certainly be out of circulation for a long time and might not work again. It would make a great deal of difference to the three doctors left, who would presumably have to divide his patients between them.

Driving to Easterwood behind the ambulance, Max was busy with the same problem. They would have to manage as best they could for a few days, but he hoped they would be able to get a suitable locum without too much delay.

Who would be in charge of the practice now that the senior partner was ill? Certainly not himself, since he was the newest member, and it was hard to imagine David Kennedy taking on the responsibility. That left only Maggie who, as the boss's daughter, had perhaps a prior claim anyway, but he doubted whether it had even occurred to her in her present state that there were important and urgent decisions to be made.

At the hospital, a huge modern building on the outskirts of the town, Dr McBride received immediate attention in the emergency department and then was whisked away to a private room. Propped up in bed, a sad figure with his misshapen mouth, he was still unconscious and totally unaware of the distress of his wife and daughter.

'I shall stay here all night,' Mrs McBride announced. 'They'll let me, won't they?' she appealed to Max.

'Oh, yes, I'm sure they will,' he said gently, and

glanced at Maggie. A little of her colour had returned, but she still looked quite unlike her usual blooming self. 'How about you?'

It had not occurred to him when he had decided to drive behind the ambulance that either of them would stay overnight which, he now realised, had been foolish. Of course they would want to stay!

'I'd like to remain too,' Maggie said, 'but I don't think I'd better. I shan't be much good for work tomorrow if I've been up all night—not that I expect to feel like it anyway,' she added sadly.

'You'll cope,' Max told her firmly, and was rewarded by a faint smile.

'You won't mind if I go home?' she asked her mother.

Mrs McBride was looking slightly reproachful. 'I'd much rather you stayed, of course, but I'm sure your father wouldn't want you to neglect the practice. The thing is, though, supposing his condition changes during the night——' her voice faltered a little '—I wouldn't want to be alone here.'

To Max it was plain enough she had really meant 'worsens' and he guessed Maggie knew it too. 'The registrar thinks there's no immediate danger,' he reminded her, 'and when Dr McBride's condition does change it will probably be for the better. At present he's stable, and no more than that can be expected for a while.'

A quiver passed over her plump face. 'I thought perhaps he was just being tactful when he said that.'

'Oh, no, I'm sure it was his medical opinion. Does that make you feel better about Maggie leaving?'

'Oh, yes, thank you.' She looked at her daughter. 'You'll ring up in the morning?'

'Of course I will, Mum.' Maggie kissed her affectionately, gave her father a long, lingering look and turned to Max. 'I'm ready now.'

At first they drove in silence. Then Maggie said emotionally, 'I'm so glad you were with us, Max. It was such a comfort to have you.'

'There was nothing anyone could do.'

'I know that, but you were able to confirm my diagnosis.' Her voice shook. 'You feel terribly unsure when it's your own father.'

'Yes, of course, I can understand that.' He stretched out his left hand and touched hers lightly in a gesture of sympathy.

Her fingers clutched feverishly at his hand and clung. 'It wasn't just having my diagnosis agreed with that I meant. It was much more than that—a sort of moral support, only that's not quite right either. I don't know what to call it, but—well, I felt less shattered as soon as I knew you were on the way.'

Max was embarrassed by her words, but he knew she was in an emotional state and therefore prone to exaggeration. In addition, they had been friends for some time, so it was only natural she should have been glad of his company at a time of family crisis. Finding it impossible to think of a suitable reply, he murmured unintelligibly and changed the subject.

'About the practice, Maggie——'

'I was thinking about that when we were riding in the ambulance. I knew that if my father were conscious he would be worrying about his patients. We shall have to get a locum, shan't we?'

Max was greatly relieved that she had made the suggestion. 'Er—will you see to it, or would you like either David or me to set the machinery in motion?'

'David won't want the responsibility, and I shall have quite enough on my plate without having that job too— which leaves you. You don't mind, do you?'

'I'll do anything to help,' he assured her.

'I knew you would.' She was still holding his hand and she now tightened her grip. 'We'll have to consult together about the actual choice of a locum,' she added in a more businesslike tone, 'but if you do the initial work that will be a big help.'

Not having an automatic car, Max required his left hand for gear change as they approached the narrow bridge at Tarling. Fortunately Maggie realised this just in time to prevent an embarrasing struggle.

When they reached the house, he got out of the car and waited while she unlocked the door.

'Is there anything more I can do?' he asked, standing in the porch. 'Get you a drink, perhaps?'

'Would *you* like one?'

'Only if you'll join me.'

Maggie looked round vaguely. The overhead light was casting deep shadows beneath her eyes and exhaustion had again removed all her normal colour. She looked at the end of her tether, and Max was overwhelmed by pity for her.

'I'll get drinks for us both,' he suggested, leading the way to the dining-room. 'I prescribe whisky—it will help you to sleep.'

He poured her a generous tot and a very small one for himself. They sipped in silence and then Max made a determined move towards the door. 'If there's nothing else I can do,' he said, 'I'll be on my way. We shall both have a lot of work to get through tomorrow.'

Maggie gulped and put down her glass with an unsteady hand. She swayed slightly as she joined him in the hall, and he wondered whether it was due to reaction, or whether the whisky had been a bit too much for her.

'Go straight up to bed,' he ordered, his hand on the door-knob, 'and be careful on the stairs. You—er—look a bit tottery to me.'

To his alarm she suddenly burst into tears and hurled herself into his arms. 'Oh, Max, I don't want to be alone,' she sobbed. 'Stay with me—please!'

CHAPTER NINE

IN THE morning Fiona awakened with a sense of foreboding. Normally she started a new week with a certain amount of pleasurable anticipation, aware that there might be difficulties, but life at the surgery would be varied and full of interest. This morning, as soon as she was properly awake, she remembered the cause of the heavy weight which lay on her spirit.

There was no doubt at all that Dr McBride's stroke would have an effect on everyone connected with the practice.

When she reached the surgery she found Maggie already there, in consultation with the receptionist.

'How is your father this morning?' Fiona asked when the conversation ended.

'There's no change. My mother spent the night at the hospital and I rang her early this morning.'

Maggie was heavy-eyed, as though she had slept badly, but her bright colour had returned and she looked almost normal. Her clothing, in two shades of green, was as unfortunate as ever, but she had taken pains with her hair and instead of straggling untidily it was fastened back with combs.

'There's a lot to be sorted out,' she went on briskly. 'I'm due over at Bedgrave today and my father should have been with me. Max will be coming instead, which leaves only David to hold the fort here, and he'll probably need some help from you.'

'I'll do all I can, of course. Will you be getting a locum?'

'Oh, yes, we couldn't possibly manage for long with only three doctors. Max is seeing to that for me.'

It must all have been arranged last night, Fiona surmised. There would have been just the two of them on the drive back from Easterwood.

Just the two of them. It was extraordnary how unwelcome she found that particular thought.

Anxious as she was to be helpful, she couldn't do much for David at first because she was occupied with a well woman clinic. This was something she had had to learn about from Liz when she'd first come to Tarling as it was outside her experience.

'People were suspicious of it at first,' Liz had told her, 'but now it's become so popular they have to hold two, one in the morning for housewives and another after working hours.'

'But what *is* it?'

'Part of it's a general check-up on health—blood-pressure, urine, weight. And then there are two very important female tests—cervical smears and breast lumps. In addition, you'll have to teach the women to inspect their own breasts monthly so that the slightest abnormality can be discovered early.'

To Fiona it made sense, and she approached her well woman clinics with a real feeling of doing something worthwhile.

Today, she worked her way steadily through those attending, finding nothing more alarming than over-weight, though this, as she pointed out, *could* be serious. Her last patient was a young woman named

Jill Newman, who usually came with her sister. Both were married to farm workers.

'Where's Shirley?' Fiona asked when she had finished her examination and found nothing wrong.

A shadow crossed Jill's attractive, healthy looking face. 'She said she was feeling a bit poorly and wouldn't bother to come today.' She hesitated, then continued, 'I don't know if I ought to say this, Nurse, but I've got a feeling there's something worrying her. We've always been close and I know her pretty well.'

'Would she tell you if there was?'

'She might, but she didn't want to talk this morning, that's for sure.'

They left it like that and, although Fiona felt vaguely dissatisfied, she put Shirley out of her mind and attended to a woman who had been having hepatitis-B injections and had come for her blood test.

It was nearly eleven-thirty and there were still people sitting in the waiting area. They surely couldn't have been so busy at Bedgrave, Fiona reasoned, and it was impossible not to wonder why Max had gone over there instead of staying in Tarling. Perhaps he didn't think Maggie would be able to cope on her own? Or had she perhaps begged for his support and he had found himself unable to refuse?

'The sooner we get a locum, the better I shall be pleased,' David said later, departing at speed, and when Fiona went out for a delayed lunch she was greeted by Anne with the same words.

'That goes for all of us, provided he—or she—is up to the job.' Fiona unwrapped her knife and fork from the paper napkin and started to eat. 'But don't imagine your troubles with appointments will be over when we do get a new doctor. I wouldn't mind betting half Dr McBride's patients will object to being seen by a stranger and will insist on having one of the regulars.'

Anne pushed a forkful of salad into her mouth. 'I'm sure you're right,' she said when she could speak, 'and I can tell you who'll be most in demand. Max.'

'Why not David or Maggie?'

'David's not so popular, and Maggie—well, men don't really like having to tell their symptoms to a girl. Of course, if she were the glamorous type some of them might enjoy it, but I'm afraid our Maggie just isn't.'

'She's very nice——'

'Oh, yes, we all know that, but what's the good of niceness when you're out to catch a man? It doesn't matter so much about being plain, but you do need a bit of style.'

'Who said anything about catching a man?' Fiona demanded.

'Nobody, but it's obvious Maggie fancies Macho Max. What we *don't* know is how he feels about her, but if he's got any sense he'll grab her and step into her father's shoes. I expect she could learn to improve her appearance in time.'

Fiona pushed a slice of cucumber round her plate and gave her full attention to spearing it. On the whole she enjoyed her lunch-hour chats with Anne, though sometimes the girl's mixture of youthful immaturity and worldly wisdom irritated her. Today she would greatly have preferred to be alone, and she told herself it was because she needed to relax after the hectic morning.

Yet when Anne had gone to do some shopping, she

still felt uptight. Wistfully, she thought back to the mood of yesterday. It had been such a happy day, right up to when the car phone had delivered its unwelcome message. Since then everything had gone awry and looked like continuing to do so. She was glad that her afternoon work occupied her full attention and not altogether sorry that she would be late getting away, since presumably there would be only one doctor to deal with the evening patients.

To her surprise Maggie appeared at five-thirty and announced that she had come to help. 'Max thought it wasn't fair to leave David on his own for both surgeries and he said he could manage alone at Bedgrave. There are never so many people as in the morning.'

'Has he been able to do anything about the locum?' Fiona asked, starting to tidy her desk.

'He did some phoning this morning and the agency said they would try and send someone tomorrow or the next day. I suppose we shall survive until then.'

She did not look as though she had had a hard day following on a bad night. Her eyes were bright and there was even an air of cheerfulness about her—which might, of course, be due to better news about her father.

'He's recovered consciousness,' she said when Fiona put her question, 'but he can't speak yet. I'm going over to the hospital when I leave here, partly to see him but also to bring my mother back. She must be terribly tired after being there nearly twenty-four hours.'

'Is it too soon to ask what the prognosis is?' Fiona ventured.

'As far as the possibility of full recovery—much too

soon. All they're prepared to say is that they're hopeful.'

Maggie went off to her father's room while Fiona continued with her tidying-up. She had nearly finished when the telephone rang and, to her surprise, it was Max.

'Have you got your car handy,' he asked briskly.

'It's at Apple Acre. I don't often bring it to——'

'Get your skates on and fetch it as quickly as you can. Then drive over here,' he ordered.

'To Bedgrave?'

'Where else?'

Sensing that he was about to hang up, Fiona prepared to do the same, but suddenly he deigned to explain.

'I'm just starting evening surgery and I've been invaded by a swarm of people with minor cuts. If we were nearer Easterwood I'd send them straight to A and E, but the injuries aren't serious and it's just not worth it. You can start on them as soon as you get here while I tackle the other patients. Hurry up.'

'What on earth's happened?' she managed to gasp before the line went dead.

'There's been a small explosion in the lab at a fertiliser factory near here. The number of people who managed to get involved is incredible.'

Fiona had been feeling depressed all day. Now, unaccountably, her spirits soared and she covered the five-minute walk to Apple Acre in record time. Bedgrave was easy to find, being on a B-road and not hidden in a tangle of lanes, but she had forgotten to ask where the surgery was.

'Opposite the Post Office. You can't miss it,' said the young woman with a pram whom she consulted.

It looked just like an ordinary house, but the brass plate told Fiona it was indeed the branch surgery. An old timber-framed building had been skilfully converted and inside it was not very different from the custom-built surgery at Tarling, except that there was no room provided for the nurse.

Fiona said, 'Hello,' to the middle-aged receptionist, who seemed to be expecting her, then looked into the waiting-room, where it was 'standing room only'. Mingling with the ordinary patients there were about a dozen pale-faced people in blood-splashed white coats, some holding bandaged hands stiffly in front of them. Relieved that there was insufficient blood to arouse her tiresome squeamishness, Fiona looked them over and came to a quick decision. She would take over the second doctor's room and begin work. No doubt the receptionist could tell her where to find what she needed.

She was on her way to the desk when Max's door opened and a patient came out. It would be only courteous to announce her arrival, Fiona reasoned, but as she put her head in she was suddenly overwhelmed by memories of last night. Consequently, when she spoke her voice came out with a horrible false brightness.

'I'm here!'

'So I see.' Max did not even glance up from a patient's card he was writing on. 'Why aren't you getting on with the job? There's plenty to do.'

This was the Max whom she had first met, the man

she had so intensely disliked. He had not spoken to her like that since her first week at Tarling.

She said indignantly, 'I'm just going to begin.'

'Tell my next patient I'm ready, will you?' was all he said in reply and, fuming, Fiona continued on her way towards the desk.

Mrs Girling, the receptionist was very ready to help, and soon Fiona was installed in the room next to Max with a plentiful supply of plasters and bandages. Although he had described the injuries as 'minor' she soon discovered that about half of them would require stitching, which meant they would have to wait until he could attend to them, but she cleaned them up, put on temporary bandages and discarded the bloodstained ones. The others kept her busy for quite a while as each of them wanted to give her a full account of the blast. By the time she had finished she felt she could have written a report on it for the local paper, but, knowing they needed to talk, she did her best to listen sympathetically.

She was busy with the last of these when Max looked in.

'Haven't you finished *yet*?' he demanded.

Fiona was tempted to answer, 'Can't you see I haven't?' but medical etiquette and the presence of the patient restrained her. With commendable self-control she ignored the unnecessary question and merely mentioned the need for stitches.

He went off again without a word and she continued with her bandaging. Reluctantly, when 'this was finished, she went to see if she could be of any assistance to Max.

She found a different doctor from the one who had

been so abrasive with her, and together they worked on the remaining casualties, Max doing the stitching and Fiona bandaging. It was impossible not to admire his gentle handling of the patients, some of whom were frankly nervous of the needle. She could only marvel at the strange way a man could change so much in such a short time.

When the waiting-room was empty and Mrs Girling, with a cheerful, 'Goodnight, doctor. You'll lock up, won't you?' had left, she glanced uncertainly at Max.

'Are you going now?'

'No such luck,' he said shortly. 'I've got some paper-work to do.'

'So have I, and a lot of tidying-up as well.'

'Better get on with it,' he told her, and disappeared into his room.

Burning with indignation, Fiona retreated into the other room and tried to concentrate on what she had to do. By now it was obvious that *she* was the one he was at odds with, and there was no possible reason for it that she could think of. She had done nothing—absolutely nothing—to put him in such a black mood.

By chance she emerged from her room, an overflow-ing waste bin clasped in her arms, at the same moment as he came out of his own. Her heart thudding, she faced him across a pile of bloodstained bandages.

Yet all she could think of to say was, 'What shall I do with these?'

'How should I know? Leave the cleaner to cope with it. It's her job.'

'OK.' Taking a deep breath to steady her nerves, Fiona summoned all her courage and made an attempt to get through to him. 'I never had a chance last

evening to thank you for taking me out to supper.
What a lovely place The Old Barn is! So different from
an ordinary restaurant.'

But she hadn't meant it to sound like that—terribly
artificial and stilted, without the slightest indication of
sincerity. No wonder the grim look on Max's face
seemed to have intensified!

He said curtly, 'It's very popular. Are you ready to
leave?'

'Yes, thank you,' she managed to answer in a small
voice.

'Then you'd better be on your way, because I want
to lock up. I've got a lot of calls to make.'

On the way back to Tarling Fiona gave herself a
severe scolding. It was only too obvious Max was
regretting last night. He had been carried away by an
amorous impulse and Dr McBride's stroke had brought
him back to earth. The way he had treated her at
Bedgrave showed that plain enough. It hadn't been just
a hint, it had been more like a slap in the face, and no
girl with any pride would tolerate that.

An overwhelming sadness was threatening to swamp
her and she had to whip up her anger to do battle with
it. There was no denying she had come very close to
being such a fool as to allow history to repeat itself.
Surely she had suffered enough over Chris without very
nearly letting the same thing happen again? Had she
already forgotten the lesson so painfully learnt?

Searching her mind for the answer, Fiona struggled
to be completely honest. She had come perilously close
to forgetting that lesson, but perhaps it wasn't too late.
She would have to steel herself, perhaps suffer some

more. . . A sob caught at her throat as another possibility occurred to her.

If Max married Maggie McBride, she knew she wouldn't be able to bear it. She would have to leave Tarling and try to find eventual happiness elsewhere. The mere thought filled her with utter dismay.

A conversation she had with Anne the following day confirmed her fear that this might possibly happen.

'I've got a juicy little piece of gossip for you,' the receptionist announced gleefully. 'At least, it might not be juicy—one shouldn't leap to conclusions, should one?—but it looks very suspicious.'

'Stop being mysterious and tell me what it is,' Fiona said lightly, without the slightest premonition that Anne's titbit would turn out to be the most painful she could possibly hear.

'You remember we were saying it would be a good idea from Max's point of view if he married Maggie? Well, it looks as though the same thing has occurred to him.'

'Don't be silly!' Fiona said sharply. 'It sticks out so far it's bound to have occurred to him, but that doesn't mean he's going to do it.'

Anne was unruffled by her comment. 'I'm not daft, Fiona, I know that. All I'm saying is that what happened on Sunday night is a pointer in that direction.'

'Dr McBride's stroke?'

'Sort of, but I really mean something which happened afterwards. My Auntie Dot lives in East Lane nearly opposite the surgery and she saw the ambulance and everything, and naturally she went across to ask what was wrong. Max was just driving off and he stopped and told her, but she could see he wasn't very pleased at being bothered just then.' She paused and took a sip of coffee.

'I still don't see what you're on about,' Fiona said impatiently.

'I'm nearly there. Later on, Max came back with Maggie but not her mother——'

'Had your Auntie Dot been looking out all that time?'

'Of course not! She just *happened* to see them. Anyway, what with all the excitement, she didn't sleep very well and she got up to make a cup of tea about two o'clock, and Max's car was just driving away. What do you think of that?'

An icy hand had clutched at Fiona's heart, squeezing it until she could have cried out with the pain. Instead she said curtly, 'I don't think anything.'

Anne looked disappointed. 'Surely it's rather significant?'

'No more than Max falling asleep at Liz Crane's house after we'd been dealing with an accident. Liz was away and I was in my own bed upstairs *alone*. Somebody saw him driving away then and started an absurd rumour. The inhabitants of Tarling must spend a lot of time looking out of the window when they should be asleep.'

'I've never heard you sound so bitchy.'

'That sort of gossip makes me feel bitchy.' Violently, she added, 'I do wish people would mind their own bloody business!'

They were silent for a moment and then, by mutual consent, changed the subject.

Later that afternoon, when Max appeared to take evening surgery, Fiona studied him covertly. He looked tired and there were lines of strain round his mouth, which told her nothing except that he was over-burdened by work.

A few minutes later he appeared suddenly in the doorway of her room. 'There's a locum coming tomorrow,' he stated baldly. 'Dr Peter Lampton.'

There were questions she would have liked to ask, such as what time the new doctor was arriving and a few personal details, but Max gave her no opportunity. He vanished as abruptly as he had come.

Dr Lampton arrived after lunch, when none of the doctors were there to greet him, and it fell to Fiona to show him round. He was a tall, thin, grey-haired man of very uncertain age. His leathery skin was apparently due to his having lived a great deal abroad, and on a warm day towards the end of June he was wearing a cardigan beneath his jacket.

'Do you often take locum jobs?' she asked when they had toured the various rooms.

'I've had several since I returned to this country, but I'm looking round for a permanency.' He gave her his nice, pleasant smile. 'I like the country, but the first essential is a golf course. Is there one near here?'

She was able to assure him on that important point, and he went on to tell her he was a widower with no family and needed only to please himself.

'That must make life very simple,' she commented.

'In a way. For instance, I'm going to put up at the inn, but a wife would certainly require something more in the nature of a hotel, and I would lose the advantage of getting to know the locals by meeting them in the bar.'

He seemed to have the right ideas, Fiona reflected as

she watched him drive off towards the Fox, and she hoped for everybody's sake that his joining the practice would benefit them all.

After his first day's work both David and Maggie expressed their satisfaction with the newcomer. She would have liked to say something easy and natural to Max about him but, owing to the restraint which had sprung up between them, found it impossible. He appeared to be getting on well with Dr Lampton, but that was all she knew about it.

Towards the end of the week something occurred which practically forced them into contact with each other.

Fiona had just got into her car with a view to taking a few prescriptions to the patients involved who, she knew, would have difficulty in collecting them from the dispensary. It was an entirely unofficial job which she sometimes performed within a small radius. She had just started the engine when Max drove up and swept into the parking space next to her. He jumped out and came straight to the open window.

'I suppose you know you've got a flat tyre?' he exclaimed sarcastically.

The wording of the question infuriated her and she flung an angry retort back at him. 'Of course I didn't know! I'm not completely crazy! Which one is it?'

'The near-side rear.'

'I couldn't see that, could I?' Almost pushing him aside, she scrambled out and went to investigate. The tyre was indeed flat.

Fiona prided herself on being able to cope with catastrophes of that sort, but she hated having to do it, all the same. With a sigh, she opened the boot to get the jack, brace and spare tyre.

'You'll never be able to undo those nuts,' Max said, almost snatching the brace out of her hand.

'Of course I can——'

'Shut up and let me get on with it,' he ordered. 'I shall be twice as quick as you.'

Standing on one side and watching his professional attack on the wheel nuts, Fiona was conscious of a slight feeling of warmth in the region of her frozen heart. They had almost come to blows, and yet they had at least been natural with each other. She would have given a great deal to know whether Max was helping her because he wanted to, or because he considered it his duty as a male. She would have liked it to be the former but feared the latter was more likely.

When he had finished Max looked at his hands in disgust. 'I'd better go and scrub up.' On the verge of flight, he suddenly turned round again. 'I almost forgot. Two items of news which would interest you.'

'Yes?' She caught her breath in fear.

'Rachel and her husband have decided to have another try at making a go of their marriage, so she's leaving Cornerways and returning to London. She wanted me to tell you.'

'That was nice of her.' It was easy to instil warmth into her voice because she was genuinely glad, but she was still wary as she reminded him, 'You said *two* items of news.'

'The other concerns the house. I've had a letter from my parents in Spain to say that the climate has done my father's chest so much good they've decided to settle there permanently. I'm to put Cornerways on the market.' He suddenly looked straight at her. 'No doubt you'll be glad. The next owners might keep the place looking more the way it was in your grandparents' day.'

The news was such a surprise that Fiona scarcely knew how to analyse her reaction to it. It seemed she was unlikely to visit there again, so the change of ownership had little significance. Besides, what Max had described as her fixation on the past seemed to be over. She was now much more concerned with the present, even though it was most unlikely to bring her happiness.

'Thanks for telling me,' she said briefly, and got into her car to make the delayed calls.

On the way back she realised she would pass the cottage where Shirley Adams lived. Her non-appearance at the clinic was still stored in the recesses of Fiona's mind, and this seemed a good opportunity to pay a casual call.

She found the girl in the kitchen, listlessly kneading pastry, and one glance at the shadowed eyes and pale face told the visitor she was still worrying about whatever it was that had kept her away from the clinic.

'Hi, Shirley!' Fiona produced a friendly smile. 'I was just passing and though I'd stop and see how you were. Are you feeling better?'

'Better?' She seemed startled. 'How could I—oh, I see what you mean. I wasn't very well earlier in the week, but I'm OK now.'

Fiona sat down without waiting for an invitation. 'Are you sure? You don't look all that fit to me.'

'I'm—I'm just tired, that's all.'

Perhaps she was pregnant, but she had only been

married a short time and that ought not to be a cause of distress, unless she had been fooling about with another man, but somehow Fiona didn't think that was likely.

There was silence, broken only by the soft sounds of pastry-making. 'You'll excuse me going on with this,' Shirley said suddenly. 'It's for Kevin's tea.'

That ought to be the cue for saying, 'I'll be on my way and let you get on with it,' but Fiona still hesitated. 'If you've got a problem you'd like to talk about to someone outside the family,' she ventured instead, 'I'm ready and willing to listen—and to help if I can.'

Shirley dropped the rolling-pin and it fell to the floor with a clatter. 'What do you mean? Why should I want to talk?' Her blue eyes met Fiona's defiantly and then, abruptly, the battle was over. 'Oh, God——' She collapsed into the nearest chair. 'I don't know what to do—I just don't know——'

Fiona was alarmed, though she kept it hidden. Fortunately there was no need for her to say anything for now the whole story came pouring out.

'It was when I was examining myself like you taught us. I found this lump, see? And I knew if I came to the clinic you'd find it too, and I tried to pretend it wasn't there, but it's no good—I can't stop thinking about it. I've got cancer, haven't I? I'm probably going to die——'

It was time to interrupt. Fiona captured one of the wildly gesticulating hands and held it firmly. 'You're much more likely to live to a ripe old age. Breast lumps are as common as—as pimples on teenagers, and most of them are harmless, only fatty tissue or cysts or something like that.'

She saw the sudden light in Shirley's eyes and hoped desperately that this story would have a happy ending. It seemed extremely likely, for, when she made her own examination, the lump was quite hard to find. Even if it was malignant, early removal would probably be the end of the matter.

'You'll have to see one of the doctors,' she explained, 'who'll make a hospital appointment for you. Which of them is your usual doctor?'

'Dr McBride, but——'

'Then you'd probably like to see Dr Maggie. I'll fix it for you and drop in again to tell you when to come.' Fiona hesitated, then added cautiously, 'You won't try to keep this from your husband, will you?'

Shirley shook her head. 'Not now I've had this talk with you. I'm ever so grateful, Nurse. I feel quite different now.'

Fiona left in a warm glow of satisfaction that made her forget the ache in her heart. But only temporarily.

CHAPTER TEN

A WEEK later Shirley's lump had been painlessly removed and proved benign, and she had nothing more to worry about.

After the recent drama, the practice seemed to have settled down into a rut which matched that in Fiona's own life. Dr Peter Lampton had fitted in well, and the patients liked him and didn't mind that he was inclined to be slow.

'Not that I wouldn't rather have the old man,' said Mrs Walsh, 'but this new chap'll do very well to be going on with.' She glanced at Fiona, who was examining a septic finger which the gardener's wife had somehow managed to acquire. '*Will* Dr McBride be back eventually?'

'We still don't know. He's a lot better than he was, but I think the most we can hope for is that he'll be able to work part-time.'

Mrs Walsh inspected her new bandage and nodded in approval. 'You'd think a doctor would look after himself, wouldn't you? He must have had high blood-pressure or something.'

'Doctors are famous for not taking care of their own health.'

'It's funny how things jog along without anything happening, and then you get one thing after another. First there was Dr McBride's stroke and then we heard the other day that Cornerways is to be sold. I wonder what the third will be.'

Would it be Maggie McBride's engagement to Max? The mental pain was worse than a physical blow, and Fiona recoiled from it with a violence which she felt must be actually visible. She said lightly, 'Does there have to be a third?'

'Things always happen in threes,' Mrs Walsh insisted. She stood up preparatory to leaving, but paused at the door. 'Have you heard whether Dr Whitmore's found a buyer for Cornerways? They say the house has been put in the hands of a posh London agent, so we may get folks who aren't used to the country and don't know anything about country ways. There's too many of those about already, to my way of thinking.'

'Dr Whitmore hasn't said anything about the prospect of selling, so I'm afraid I can't answer your question.'

He hadn't said anything to her at all except on matters connected with the practice, and the continued restraint between them was breaking her heart.

'It seems rum to me he doesn't buy it off his parents himself,' Mrs Walsh was saying. 'He'll need somewhere to live.'

'It's too big for one man,' Fiona pointed out unwisely.

'There's a rumour going round that he's thinking of getting married to Dr Maggie. With two of them working they'd be able to afford a place like that quite easy.'

When the patient had gone Fiona resolutely put the whole of the conversation out of her mind and concentrated on other matters. But it returned to haunt her as soon as she went home. Glad of something to do, she was pleased to be asked to help with raspberry picking after supper.

They talked spasmodically as they worked and Fiona's tortured mind and heart began to relax a little. But unfortunately Liz introduced the subject of Max.

'Has he said anything to you about his sister's reflexology treatment?' she asked.

'Not recently, but I know he was very annoyed about it.'

'And even more annoyed, I suppose, when I cured her.' Liz popped a ripe berry into her mouth. 'I do think it's ridiculously obstinate of him not to admit that reflexology can work miracles.'

'He said something to me once about it being all in the mind.'

'Fiddlesticks!' Liz snapped. 'You can't put a strained shoulder right by treating the patient's mind. I do think he might give credit where credit's due, don't you?'

'I certainly do,' Fiona agreed with unnecessary fervour.

At that moment the Labrador, who had been lying stretched out, raised her head and looked towards the house. At the same moment they became aware that the telephone was ringing. Liz went off at a trot and Fiona continued her picking.

'It's for you,' she reported when she returned. 'Dr Max. It's strange we were just talking about him.'

'I do hope it's not an accident. He didn't say?'

'He was in one of his curt moods.'

As Fiona neared the house her steps grew slower. It was such a lovely evening, she didn't want to set off to some scene of horror, not even with Max. She didn't want to go *anywhere* with him, she told herself firmly, knowing all the time it wasn't true.

It was not an accident.

'Are you busy just now?' Max asked when she picked up the receiver.

'Yes. I'm picking raspberries.'

'That's not being busy.'

'You ought to try it, then. It's back-breaking work.'

'Well, at least you've got someone handy who can put you right if you do damage your back.'

Hating his sarcasm, Fiona retorted, 'I'm sure you didn't ring up to talk about reflexology. What *did* you want?'

'To ask you to come out for a drink.' And, as her pulses started racing, he added, 'I've got something to tell you.'

'Oh!' Her voice, though she was unaware of it, was full of dismay. Mrs Walsh's assertion that things always went in threes flashed into her head. Was this the third? And yet, if he and Maggie were about to announce their engagement, why should Max inform her— Fiona—about it in advance?

'I don't think I'll come,' she said flatly.

'Please. . .' He was actually sounding quite humble. 'It really is important and I don't want to tell you over the phone. We needn't have a drink if you don't want to. We could just sit somewhere and talk.'

Fiona didn't much like the sound of that either, but perhaps it might be less false than a semi-social occasion in a pub. Anyway, to have the stubborn, stiff-necked Max actually pleading with her was so extra-ordinary she felt herself weakening.

'OK,' she said shortly. 'I'll expect you in five minutes.'

Upstairs, she attended rapidly to her hair and face, and made sure her pink, patterned summer dress was not raspberry-stained. Just as she was ready she heard a car outside and she ran downstairs with fast-beating heart.

Max had got out and was holding open the door. She slipped in without a word but, just for a moment, their eyes met and clung. Trying to read the expression in his, Fiona failed dismally. He didn't look like a man about to announce exciting news. If it hadn't been utterly crazy she would have said the vivid blue eyes held a deep and hopeless sadness.

Without speaking he drove to the same spot on the Heath where they had stopped before. The families had all gone home and the lovers were waiting for dusk, so it was as deserted as last time. Switching off the engine, Max leaned his arms on the steering-wheel, staring straight ahead.

'I'm afraid I've got rather a shock for you,' he said. 'I wanted to tell you before you heard it casually from someone else.'

Her breathing almost stopped and she had a choking sensation. He was going to tell her he was engaged to Maggie—what else could he possibly mean?

She said, 'Yes?' so faintly that it barely reached him even in that confined space. His nearness was an intoxication and a torture to her. Her body yearned for contact with his, and at the same time she pressed herself against the door to limit the chances of a casual touch which would set her on fire.

Max seemed to have difficulty in finding the right

words. They were both so still that a blackbird came and perched on the car bonnet, gave them a puzzled look and flew away. In the distance sheep were bleating monotonously.

Fiona found her courage. 'I can't imagine what you've brought me here to talk about,' she said sharply, 'which couldn't just as well have been discussed at Apple Acre, but now that we're here why don't you get on with it?'

He stopped frowning into space and gave her a quick glance before looking away again. 'I was trying to think of the best way of breaking the news, but I'm not much of a diplomat, so I'll plunge straight into it. You know, of course, that Cornerways is up for sale?'

It was the last thing she had expected him to say, but she managed to gasp out, 'You told me so——' before he went hurrying on as though relieved to have got started at last.

'I put it in the hands of several agents, including one in London, and quite a number of people have been to look round, but nobody actually made an offer until a couple of days ago. The London agent phoned to tell me this chap was driving down, and they asked me to be sure I was there to receive him as he seemed very keen. Well, you can imagine how inconvenient it was under present circumstances, but I managed it somehow, and he turned up last evening.'

'I really can't think why you're telling me all this,' Fiona said.

'You'll understand when you know the name of the prospective purchaser.' Max turned to face her. 'This is where the shock comes in, so brace yourself. The man's name was Shelton.'

It was more of a surprise than a shock. Fiona was startled, certainly, but she quickly rallied. 'It's not an uncommon name.'

'Perhaps not, but there's more to come. During the course of conversation he told me he was seriously looking for a house in the country and when he heard of Cornerways he felt he had to come and look at it.' He paused and then added quietly, 'He was your father, Fiona.'

She could feel the blood draining from her face. Her hands were suddenly icy cold and she shivered. He was right—it had been a most terrible shock, and there was no way he could have made it any less.

'Did—did you mention me?' she managed to ask.

He shook his head. 'I didn't feel I had the right. It's for you to say whether you want to meet him or not. I expect you'd like time to think about that?'

'Well—yes, I would—think about it, I mean. For years I blamed him for walking out on my mother, but now I'm fully adult I realise that the break-up of the marriage was probably at least as much her fault.' She sat brooding, unconsciously twisting her hands together nervously, and then asked suddenly, 'What's he like, Max?'

'In appearance? Tall and slim like you, with plenty of hair still——'

'Grey?'

'It's hard to tell. Perhaps silver-blond would be a good description of it.'

'He was always wildly good-looking and I admired him tremendously when I was a child, even though he wasn't the sort of father who enjoyed juvenile company.'

'What did he do for a living in those days?'

'He was in advertising and very much a town person. I simply can't imagine him living in the country. Was he *really* serious about buying the house?'

'Oh, yes, I think so.' Max paused, apparently again searching for the right words. 'There's something I haven't told you. Your father was not alone. He brought his fiancée with him—a nice woman named Barbara—and she's dead keen on country life, which is part of the reason for the move from London. . .'

It was all too much. Fiona had scarcely rallied after the first shock before she received the second, and for a moment she simply stopped listening. When she tuned in again Max was explaining the other reason why her father wanted to leave the city.

'He's still in advertising, but apparently he feels the rat-race is shortening his life, and he doesn't want that with a new wife in the offing. Consequently he's sold his agency for a thumping big sum and intends to do a bit of freelancing.'

'He didn't have his own agency when—when he left my mother, but certainly he always worked very hard.'

'He's a very successful man, Fiona. There's no doubt about that.'

She said in a low voice, 'My mother is successful too, a real high-powered businesswoman. It's funny I'm so different, isn't it?'

'Neither of them seems to have been particularly clever in personal matters,' Max pointed out.

'Are you suggesting *I* am?' Fiona turned on him angrily, using her indignation to mask the feelings concealed beneath it. Desperately she longed to hurl herself into his arms, to find comfort in their shelter and perhaps even fulfilment when his body responded to the contact with hers. If it did.

Max seemed unaware of the barely controlled emotion. 'Only you can answer that,' he said bleakly, but in spite of the coolness of his tone, he put out his hand and gently touched hers. 'Do you want to go back to your fruit picking now?'

'Yes, please,' she said in a small voice.

But Fiona was not destined to help Liz any more that evening.

They had just left the Heath and were driving between cultivated fields when Max braked sharply. A woman had run out, apparently from a parked car, and was gesticulating to them to stop. As he halted and wound down the window she came rushing up in a state of great agitation.

'I've just seen a most dreadful sight! I was driving along quite slowly and I noticed a tractor in that field——' she turned and pointed '—and just as I looked at it I saw it tip right over, like it was into a ditch. I didn't know what to do—oh, please, do come and help!'

Max wasted no time. He said curtly to Fiona, 'Come on—let's have a look.'

She followed him without question as he forced a way through the hedge, though her legs were trembling and there was a cold, sick feeling in her stomach. The tractor lay on its side only a few yards away, its enormous wheels motionless against the evening sky and the driver's cab almost out of sight in a deep ditch.

What of the man trapped in there? Fiona's imagination was tormenting her as she pictured what his injuries might be, but she thrust aside her fears as Max began to climb up the huge vehicle and struggled to open the door. To her immense relief he was successful, and she called out, 'Shall I come up too?'

'Hang on a bit until I've assessed the situation.'

Only too glad to do so, she waited until he had made a brief examination.

'He's out cold,' he reported a moment later, 'and I reckon he's probably got fractures on his left side. If this had been one of the old-type tractors without a cab, he'd very likely have been killed.'

'Will the firemen have to be sent for?'

'Oh, no, the ambulance chaps are experts at getting people out of awkward places.' Max, his trousers stained with oil and mud and his shirt filthy, looked down at her. 'Run back to my car, there's a good girl, and phone for an ambulance, and when you've done that you can bring me my emergency bag.'

The woman who had witnessed the accident was waiting anxiously in the road and seemed relieved that she could now shelve the responsibility and drive on. Carrying the heavy bag, Fiona returned to the field. To her surprise Max had his head in the cab and was talking to his patient.

'How is he?' she ventured, handing up the bag.

'Conscious and in pain. I want to give him a shot of morphine. You rang the ambulance service?'

'Of course I did.' And she couldn't resist adding, 'I always do what I'm told.'

He scowled at her and she felt ashamed of her levity. He wouldn't know it was due to her aversion to accidents.

'My wife. . .' the injured man murmured faintly. 'She'll be expecting me home——'

'That'll be Poplar Farm,' Max said. 'Mrs Wilson?'

'That's right.'

'The nurse will drive there and break the news. You can depend on her to do it tactfully.' He tossed down the keys which Fiona had returned to him with the medical bag. 'I expect you'll be glad of something to do,' he added unexpectedly.

Fiona was, but she would not have chosen this particular duty. She spent a moment familiarising herself with the controls of the car and then drove on slowly until she found a farm road. As she followed it towards a distant farmhouse, she tried to plan what she should say, then decided to wait and see what Mrs Wilson was like.

She turned out to be young, with a baby in her arms. Desperately sorry for her, Fiona did her best to make the accident sound less horrific than it really was.

'Oh, my God!' The dark-haired girl collapsed into a chair. 'I've always been afraid of this happening—I dunno why, but I really have.'

'And now it's happened and it could have been so much worse, and one thing's for sure—your husband will be extra careful in future.'

'But he won't be able to work for ages, and what'll we do?'

Not knowing the answer to that, Fiona attempted none and instead offered to hold the baby while his mother collected a few necessities for her husband and got ready to come with her.

'Have you any animals that will require attention?' Fiona asked.

'The dogs and cats and chickens have all been fed. They'll be OK till I get back.' Mrs Wilson had apparently pulled herself together very creditably. 'I suppose it's no good asking how long I'm likely to be at the hospital?'

'I'm afraid not. Dr Whitmore seemed to think there may be fractures which will require a spell in the operating theatre, so you may be able to get home as soon as you know what the injuries are.'

'I'll ring up my dad. He's a farmer too and I expect he'll probably be able to help with the farm.' She sat silent for a moment, trying to grapple with the future, and then gave up. 'I can't seem to think past what's happening now.' Her voice trembled.

'That's only natural, but I'm sure you'll find people will rally round.'

They arrived at the scene only a few minutes before the ambulance. In spite of her distress, Fiona was fascinated by the skilful way the two men, helped by Max, extracted their patient from his difficult position. He had lapsed again into unconsciousness and his wife stood quietly watching, occasionally wiping her eyes but otherwise calm.

'They're a nice young couple,' Max said sadly as they resumed their interrupted drive back to Apple Acre. He slowed down on the outskirts of Tarling and approached the bridge with caution. 'You'll let me know what decision you come to about meeting your father, won't you?'

Fiona had almost forgotten her problem and was surprised to find she had come to a decision. 'I've already made up my mind I ought to meet him. It would be ridiculous, if he does buy Cornerways, for us to be living within a mile or so of each other and not communicate. He'd be bound to hear about my existence sooner or later and the situation would be that much more difficult if I'd ignored him. Of course, if he doesn't go through with the purchase, there'll be no problem. I shall stay out of his life the way I've always done.'

'Seems a pity,' Max said thoughtfully. 'I've rather got the impression you don't have much contact with your mother either.'

'No, I don't.' Her eyes challenged him to comment further, but all he said was, 'I'll let you know what happens,' and drew up at Apple Acre.

Two days later Max told her that there was good news about the tractor driver, who was expected to make a complete recovery, though it would be some time before he could work again. As well, he announced that the purchase by Colin Shelton of Cornerways had been confirmed and the legal machinery set in motion. He and Barbara were coming down to Tarling the following week to talk about curtains and carpets.

'Have you told him anything? About me, I mean,' Fiona asked nervously.

Max shook his head. 'How would it be if you came over for drinks?'

'You surely don't expect me to walk in and say brightly, "Hello, Dad! Long time no see!" You're crazy! He might even have second thoughts about buying the house if he knew I was around.'

Max looked startled. 'You're not serious? I can't see why it should make the slightest difference. Anyway, there was no need for you to jump to the conclusion that I wasn't going to give him prior warning of the awful fact that he'd got a daughter in the neighbourhood. I shouldn't dream of it.'

'I'm sorry—I'm not thinking very straight just now,' Fiona apologised. 'I wonder how we shall get on. It's possible I shall be the one who can't face up to the situation, and if that happens I shall have to find another job as far away from Tarling as can be managed.'

If she had been looking at Max instead of speaking with her eyes fixed on a bowl of roses on her desk, she would have seen a shutter come down over his face, making it impossible to guess his reaction to her statement. He made no verbal comment either, but she was so absorbed in trying to recover from the glimpse of a bleak future which she had unveiled that she scarcely noticed.

With an effort she roused herself and went on speaking. 'Please break the news to my father, Max— and his girlfriend. It's only fair to give them notice so they can avoid me if they want to. I won't come to Cornerways if you don't promise.'

'Very well, but personally I don't think you've anything to worry about.'

Left alone, Fiona sat still and took a few deep breaths in an effort to calm herself. It was ridiculous to feel so worked up when she had another whole week to get through before her ordeal, and besides, it might turn out not to be an ordeal at all but a pleasure!

The arrival of the hospital van, which called daily to collect specimens for analysis in the path lab, claimed her attention, and by the time she had handed them

over and agreed with the driver's weather forecast—
that it was going to rain—she had recovered her poise.

It did rain too, beginning just as she was starting to
walk home, coming down in huge drops which rapidly
soaked through her light summer clothing. The cool
water on her face and body was wonderfully refreshing
and she arrived feeling cleansed and exhilarated.

During the next few days her mood remained stable,
but as the meeting with the father whom she had not
seen since she was a child drew nearer, her nervousness
returned in full measure. From Max's description it
sounded as though he was still sexually attractive and
he might be going to marry a younger woman, who
would be dismayed at being introduced to a grown-up
stepdaughter. Supposing Barbara didn't like her?

'Have you told him about me?' Fiona demanded as
Max passed her on his way to start his morning calls on
the day of the drinks party.

He was apparently absorbed in problems of his own
and he stared at her blankly as she put her question.

'Told who? What are you talking about?' he flung at
her over his shoulder.

'My father, of course.' She was hurt that he seemed
to have forgotten.

'No, I haven't.' He held up his hand to forestall her
indignant outburst. 'I've decided it would be better to
leave it until he gets here——'

'But supposing he doesn't want to meet me?'

'Don't be silly—of course he will. But in the unlikely
event of his refusing, I'll give you a ring.'

He was gone, and Fiona was obliged to be content,
though she found it extremely difficult. At the end of
the afternoon, when Max was still seeing patients, she

could not resist looking into his room before she went home, choosing a moment between two patients.

'You won't forget to let me know if I'm not to come?' she begged.

He looked up from the card he was filling in and frowned. 'I don't know what's come over you, Fiona, making a ridiculous fuss like this.'

'It isn't ridiculous to me. You *will* remember?'

'OK. Send the next patient in, will you?'

She turned away to summon the patient, whom she had believed to be standing a little way behind her, waiting for their conversation to end. But it wasn't the man with the hacking cough who stood there—he was still sitting down. It was Maggie, and she had obviously heard every word.

The two girls looked at each other. Both had brown eyes; Fiona's were a beautiful velvety brown, not unlike the darkest pansies, but Maggie's were muddier and less expressive. There was some sort of emotion visible in them now, though, and to Fiona it looked very like bewilderment.

Embarrassed, she moved away. There was a sharp click and the door of Max's room closed behind his partner, leaving the patient still waiting. No doubt Maggie wanted a quick consulation about one of her cases, Fiona reasoned, but the incident left her feeling oddly distressed.

At Apple Acre she was very quiet throughout supper, and Liz, understanding the reason, left her alone. Afterwards she had far too much time for getting ready and for changing her mind about what she was going to wear. She wanted to look sophisticated but was aware that her taste in clothes tended to be simple.

She had been asked for drinks, which warranted a certain amount of 'dressing up' but, on the other hand, her father and Barbara would have come prepared only to discuss curtains and carpets.

Eventually she chose a plain black linen skirt, calf-length, and teamed it with a simple vivid green top with a low neck. Although she usually wore her hair down when she wasn't working, this evening she brushed it until it shone and then twisted it up again with so much care that it fitted her head like a golden cap. Fairly satisfied, she went downstairs to show herself to Liz.

'Very nice.' Liz nodded in approval. 'You're lucky being tall, you can carry things off so well. Your father ought to be proud of you.'

Fiona's lightly made-up face crinkled into a grimace. 'I just want to keep my end up, that's all. This Barbara woman may be very smart, for all I know, even if she does like the country.' She glanced at her watch. 'It's nearly time to leave and I haven't heard anything from Max.'

'That means it's OK, doesn't it?'

'But he might have been delayed by an emergency or something. Perhaps he hasn't even got home yet.'

'For heaven's sake, Fiona!' Liz exploded. 'You really are being absurd. Pull yourself together and get in your car and *go*!'

Fiona smiled tremulously, then broke into a laugh as Bella the Labrador padded up to her, sniffed suspiciously at the black skirt and turned away again.

'She prefers me in jeans,' she said, 'and I don't blame her.' Picking up her car keys, she waved a would-be nonchalant hand and went out to face her ordeal.

CHAPTER ELEVEN

IT WAS the first time Fiona had used her car to get to Cornerways and the distance, which took a good twenty minutes to walk, slipped by at alarming speed. In a way, she would have preferred to walk this evening as the gentle exercise might have calmed her nerves, but she was anxious to appear without a hair out of place. Besides, her high-heeled sandals were quite unsuitable.

There was a car outside the house, an expensive dark blue Rover. Looking at it as she parked, Fiona told herself it belonged to her own father. It should have been dear and familiar instead of as strange as a brand-new car in a motor salesroom. Pushing the thought aside, she marched up the garden path with head held high and a fast-beating heart.

Max opened the door. He wore beautifully creased trousers and a cream shirt with a hospital tie and gold cuff-links. 'Wow!' His blue eyes twinkled at her. 'You've certainly got yourself up to make an impression, but I wish you'd worn your hair down. I like it better that way.'

'It's not you I'm trying to impress,' she retorted.

He laughed and ushered her into the sitting-room before she had time to remember she was on the verge of panic. She entered with aplomb, but just inside the door she came to an involuntary halt.

A tall man in a lightweight summer suit stood facing her, a glass in his hand. He was exactly as Max had described him—slim, good-looking with a plentiful supply of silver-blond hair. Her memory of him was hazy, and yet she felt she would have known him anywhere, he had altered so little.

Was he unaltered in other ways? she couldn't help wondering—still over-fond of women, inclined to be conceited about his looks and impatient of family life?

They looked at each other in silence for a brief moment and then each moved towards the other. Fiona offered her hand, intending a quick, formal shake which would show him she intended to play it cool, but she found it taken in a warm, firm clasp and held on to.

'Well, daughter?' Colin Shelton smiled down into her eyes. 'This is indeed a pleasure, and one I've waited a long time for.'

She wanted to say caustically, 'There was no need for you to wait. You only had to make the first move,' but in the face of such charm she found it impossible. What did it matter anyway? The past was over, and only the future would show whether he had changed more than appeared on the surface.

With a sudden unexpected surge of emotion, she hoped with all her heart that he had. She needed somebody in her life whom she could love and know that that love was returned. Needed it desperately. And so she said slowly, 'We've both waited a long time,' and gave him a small, tremulous smile.

They had been standing in the middle of the room, so absorbed in each other that Fiona had actually momentarily forgotten the presence of a stranger. She was reminded by her father.

'I want you to meet my fiancée.' Still holding her hand, Colin drew her towards the open french windows where a woman had been standing silently. 'Barbara, my dear,' he went on, 'I'm very happy to introduce the long-lost Fiona.'

Long-lost indeed! Stifling a slight bitterness, Fiona gave her full attention to her prospective stepmother.

Barbara was a considerable surprise. She looked several years younger than Colin, not because of any attempt to appear so but because she really was, and was clearly not the sort of woman to pretend. She wore a brown and white summer dress, and her brown hair was cut with a neat fringe above rather beautiful grey-blue eyes. Her skin was good and she had a lovely smile, but she had allowed herself to get just a little overweight. The result was a comfortable, almost motherly figure and an air of tolerance and calm.

She was as different from Fiona's mother as anyone could possibly be.

'You're so like your father!' Barbara greeted her cheerfully. She was obviously quite unimpressed by the drama of the occasion; she simply accepted it. 'Max has been telling us all about your coming to Tarling because of this house, and that, of course, is what drew Colin to it in the first place.'

Finding her host had put a glass into her hand, Fiona sipped appreciatively. 'Do you like Cornerways?' she asked.

'Oh, *yes*! It's just the sort of house I've always wanted. I was brought up in the country, like Colin, but I've lived most of my life in London. Incidentally, I've also got an unhappy marriage behind me. It's wonderful to think we're going to opt out of the rat-race and settle down here together.'

Fiona glanced over her shoulder and found her father

deep in conversation with Max. There was no reason why she shouldn't remain where she was and listen to Barbara's praise of the house, the village and the entire countryside. It made pleasant hearing and she was in agreement with all of it. She found herself describing incidents in her childhood holidays at Cornerways which no one had cared to listen to since.

'You must come and see us often,' Barbara finished earnestly, 'and get to know your father all over again.'

Fiona murmured something. At that moment the prospect appealed to her enormously. To have a home again, somewhere she could drop in without an invitation and not have to be on her best behaviour. Emotion welled up in her at the mere thought of it and for a moment her eyes were misty.

Then the dream vanished—a lot had to happen before she could ever find herself in that happy situation. The completion of the sale had to take place, the wedding, the move from London and the settling in. Above all, she herself had to find out whether she could bear to remain at Tarling if Max married the doctor's daughter.

The two men were talking about practical details concerning the house and Barbara was drawn into the discussion. The three of them moved outside to look at something for a moment and Fiona was alone in Rachel's over-perfect room. Would Max keep this furniture, she wondered, and move it to wherever he intended to live? It wouldn't make a very suitable background for Maggie!

Why did her thoughts keep returning to the same subject? She really ought to have better control over them. Scolding herself, she moved across to study a strange-looking picture hanging on the opposite wall, a blur of red and orange which presumably represented something, but she couldn't think what it was.

The others came back at that moment and Barbara joined her in her study. 'Whatever is it?' she asked, and they both laughed.

The remainder of the evening passed quickly, since no one wanted to be late. Colin and his fiancée had to drive to their hotel at Easterwood, Max still had a few calls to make, and Fiona was so full of turbulent thoughts and feelings that she knew she needed to be alone for a while.

The two older people drove off first, and as soon as they were out of sight round the corner, Fiona made a dive for her own car.

'Well?' Max asked, looking down at her through the open window. And when she did not immediately reply, he added, 'Are you happy, Fiona?'

'Happy?' The question startled her and she couldn't think how to answer it. Supposing she said, 'I'll never be happy until you love me the way I love you'? Would he be embarrassed? Appalled? Whatever was likely to be the effect of such a statement, Fiona had no intention of making it.

She said lightly, 'I think the evening might be considered a success, don't you? I'm certainly happy my father is marrying Barbara.'

She could feel him looking at her, but she kept her eyes resolutely fixed ahead. Consequently she was taken by surprise when he suddenly opened the door she had only just closed, caught her by the shoulders and literally dragged her out of the car. She made no resistance and, so great was his strength, it would have probably been useless anyway. Before she knew what was happening she found herself folded in his arms, and the experience was so wonderful she had absolutely no desire to put an end to it.

Max said thickly, 'I've been longing to do this all the evening. You looked so lovely, I could hardly keep my hands off you.'

She began despairingly, 'Oh, Max, you shouldn't——' and then his mouth silenced the protest and she closed her eyes and gave herself up to the utter bliss of knowing that the barriers which had divided them had come down. For the moment.

It ended far too soon. He released her as abruptly as he had snatched her, and she almost fell back against the car.

'Did you say I shouldn't?' he asked, and his voice held a bitterness that extinguished Fiona's fragile happiness like the flame of a candle. 'God—how right you are! You'd better go home, Fiona, before I pick you up and carry you back into the house and make love to you. Go on—get in the car and drive away, back to your reflexologist friend. She's got a pretty low opinion of me, and if you tell her about my recent behaviour, no doubt I shall sink even lower.'

Fiona tried to say, 'I wouldn't dream of telling Liz,' but the words stuck in her throat. Through a mist of tears she started the engine and turned the car with a horrible grinding of gears quite unusual with her. The hedges flashed past as she rattled down the lane, but by the time she reached the road she had got a grip on herself and was driving normally. It would be stupid to have an accident just because Max had kissed her and then rejected her in the plainest possible way, making it perfectly clear that, although she attracted him physically, he had no further use for her.

It wasn't very complimentary to a girl to be wanted for her body alone, and Fiona burned with rage at the insult. By the time she reached Apple Acre indignation had dried her tears and she had more or less recovered her composure.

'How did it go?' Liz asked.

'Fine! I like the woman my father is going to marry very much indeed, and I think he and I will get on all right. At present I'm just a bit scared of his good looks and charm.'

'I expect you get your own good looks from him.'

'Meaning I'm missing out on the charm?' Somehow Fiona managed to laugh.

'Meaning nothing of the sort. There'd be no sense in turning it on when you're with me—it'd be entirely wasted. You're completely natural at Apple Acre, and that's the way I like it.'

Later, sitting at the table, sipping a bedtime drink, Fiona reflected sadly that if she hadn't inherited her father's attractiveness Max would have probably continued to treat her in the abrasive way he had done at the beginning, in which case she would certainly not have fallen in love with him so disastrously.

And yet when you loved somebody like that it was just about impossible to wish it hadn't happened.

That night she lay thinking in bed for a long time. Happy memories of her childhood mingled with the evening at Cornerways which unrolled like a film, and all of it mixed up with her love for Max and the distress it was causing her. Her pillow was hot and her head felt like bursting, and eventually she got up, took a cool drink of water and some paracetamol, and at last fell asleep.

The next day it was made abundantly plain that Max had reverted to a formal doctor-and-nurse relationship. No doubt he was regretting his lapse last night and wanted to make it clear it had been a momentary aberration.

Two could play at that game, and Fiona determined to beat him even if her heart was breaking. In their brief encounters she was cool and poised, she said, 'Yes, Doctor,' and 'No, Doctor,' and ignored the puzzled glances he occasionally gave her.

'Max is like a bear with two sore heads these days,' Anne complained. 'Do you think something's gone wrong with his romance with Maggie?'

'We don't know for sure there ever was any romance,' Fiona pointed out.

'He stayed the night with her, didn't he? Well, part of the night anyway.'

'That doesn't mean a thing.'

Anne looked thoughtful. 'I rather think that with a girl like Maggie it would have to. She's old-fashioned in many ways, and her parents too.'

At the end of the month Dr McBride came home, walking slowly with a stick and still slurring his words but otherwise enormously improved. It was hoped he would eventually make an almost complete recovery, and the whole village shared in his family's rejoicing. Although she was as delighted as anyone, Fiona got weary of discussing it with patients who were all determined to regard his recovery as a miracle. There seemed little point in reminding them how very efficiently strokes were handled these days.

Things were happening in her own life too. Barbara came down to Tarling by herself and stayed at a guesthouse in the village. She was full of news.

'We're moving into Cornerways about the middle of August,' she told Fiona, 'but the reason I'm here now is because I want to go through the furniture with Max and decide which, if any, items we want to buy. Colin has given me a free hand.' Her eyes twinkled. 'He's not very interested in domestic matters.'

'What's going to happen to the furniture you don't want? Surely Max will keep some of it for his own use?'

'He doesn't seem to have that intention. I don't think he likes it very much.'

'Do you happen to know where he intends to live?' Fiona couldn't resist asking.

Barbara gave her a puzzled look. 'Hasn't he told you? Somehow I got the impression you knew each other quite well.'

'We've been out together a few times, that's all. He doesn't discuss his future plans with me.'

'I see.'

Fiona had an uncomfortable feeling her future stepmother saw rather more than she'd been intended to, and she was relieved when Barbara went on to answer the question in a less meaningful tone.

'Max intends to take his time over finding a suitable smallish house, and in the meantime he's been invited to stay with the McBrides, whose house, apparently, is quite roomy. I'm not at all sure he thinks it's a good idea, because it's right next to the surgery and it'll be like living over the shop.'

Fiona had hidden her dismay with swiftly veiled eyes. She hoped her expression gave away as little. 'I would have thought he'd prefer to stay at the Fox, like Dr Lampton.'

'Perhaps they haven't got a room. It's quite a small pub, isn't it? Anyway, apparently Dr McBride and his wife are keen on the idea, and I don't suppose Max wanted to upset either of them just now. He's so kind and thoughtful—it'd be just like him to go along with whatever they wanted.'

Did that also include marrying their daughter? The question leapt into Fiona's mind before she could strangle it at birth. It remained to torment her so that she entirely missed what Barbara said next and, when she resurfaced, was quite surprised to find they were discussing the wedding.

'We wanted it to be at Tarling church, but the fact that we're both divorced has made difficulties. So the actual ceremony will be at the register office in Easterwood, and then we're having a short service of blessing at the church. There's no need for you to go all the way to Easterwood, but we'll definitely want you at the service.'

'Just try and keep me away!' Fiona smiled with genuine warmth. 'Shall I be the only person there?'

'Oh, no, we've got a few friends coming down from London—*real* friends, I mean, and the rector seems to think there may be some of the older Tarling people who remember Sheltons at Cornerways in the days of Colin's youth.'

'Like Mr and Mrs Walsh,' Fiona said, then had to explain who they were.

'I hope George will continue to come,' said Barbara.

'I like gardening myself, but I've no illusions about Colin's enthusiasm—it just doesn't exist—and I shall need some help.'

They went on talking about small, happy, domestic matters and finally separated with the pleasant feeling that they had become good friends. Unfortunately, as soon as Fiona was alone again she began to worry about the significance of Max going to live with the McBrides. What was the *real* reason? It might, of course, be the one Barbara had suggested, and with all her heart she hoped it was.

The day of the wedding was warm and sunny after a period of rain, and the gardens, windowboxes and hanging baskets of Tarling were a blaze of summer colour. The heavy scent of roses hung in the air as Fiona drove to the church, and the small dark leaves of the box hedges in the churchyard glistened in the sunlight as she walked between crazily leaning tombstones.

Inside the church it was dark and cool, with muted sunshine filtering through the ancient stained glass. Her father and Barbara were in the front pew, the bride looking very attractive in a soft yellow dress and smart white hat, and behind them about a dozen total strangers talked quietly among themselves. Further back a handful of villagers, including the Walshes, sat silently waiting for the service to begin. On an impulse Fiona slipped in beside George and his wife who, though obviously surprised, welcomed her with beaming smiles. She sat very still, absorbing the beauty and peace of her surroundings and sending up a small, involuntary prayer that these two might find the happiness in their new marriage which had been denied them hitherto.

She was standing up, an open hymn book in her hand but still wrapped up in her own private world, when she felt someone else slide into the pew. Max had joined her.

Her mood of exaltation and strange calm was instantly shattered and she felt the colour suffusing her face. She kept her eyes on her book, but she could hear him singing lustily. He had a pleasant baritone voice and appeared to be enjoying himself. When the hymn ended he sat with his sleeve just touching her bare arm and she could not move away without making it obvious.

Fiona heard no more of the service. She was too busy concentrating on making a decision which she had been putting off for far too long.

When the service was over she moved swiftly away and joined the little crowd round the bridal couple, acknowledging introductions with a brittle gaiety which everyone appeared to accept as natural, smiling at all and sundry until her face felt as though it might split, and chatting animatedly to the rector about something or other, though afterwards she had no recollection of what they had said to each other.

Max had disappeared. Presumably he had hurried back to his patients.

At Cornerways, during the next two hours, Fiona concentrated totally on the present and acted as she had never acted before. Over and over again, each time with a different audience, she went through the drama of her coming to Tarling and later on finding her father had done the same thing, each of them being drawn by the house in which the party was now taking place.

'And you hadn't seen each other for years and years? It must have been wonderful meeting again after so long!' people said, varying the actual wording slightly. 'You must be so happy to think you'll be able to see plenty of each other in the future,' the more sentimental usually added.

'But we *aren't* going to see plenty of each other!' Fiona wanted to scream back at them. 'I shan't be here after I've worked out my month's notice.'

The way she had felt when Max unexpectedly joined her in church had defeated her at last. She had desperately wanted to remain in Tarling and had tried hard to convince herself she would be able to stand it, but it was no good. And one of the worst aspects of it was that people would inevitably connect her departure with the coming of her father and his new wife.

It was nothing to do with them at all. In fact, they were one of the reasons she wanted to stay, but nobody would believe that unless she set the record straight by telling the truth—which was clearly impossible.

The party seemed to go on forever, but at last people began to talk about the long drive back to London, and eventually to take their leave. When everyone had gone, Fiona was pressed to stay a little longer, and laughingly refused.

'You two will want to start your honeymoon,' she joked, and was not surprised when the corny remark was ignored.

It was an immense relief to feel the cool night air on her flushed face and she decided to drive round for a while before returning to Apple Acre. There was a lot of planning to be done. First of all she must decide what excuse she could give for moving on again so soon after her arrival, and one thing was for sure. Whatever she managed to dredge up was certain to be unsatisfactory.

Pondering deeply, she drove aimlessly round the country roads, encountering very little traffic and her in-built automatic pilot attending to it competently when she did happen to meet another vehicle. After twenty minutes or so she found herself again approaching Tarling without any of her problems solved, and she was suddenly so tired she couldn't think any more.

Before her lay the narrow bridge with its warning sign of two arrows, one black, one red. Everybody knew that meant cars driving into the village had right of way, and those coming out were supposed to wait for them, but in practice people tended to work out their own method, which meant that those arriving at the bridge first took precedence.

Tonight Fiona, who had right of way, slowed down and looked to see if there was another car in the offing. Seeing an empty street, she started to cross. At that moment a big car came out of a side turning without pausing, made straight for the bridge and, apparently oblivious of the smaller Metro, continued at unabated speed.

Blinding, undipped headlights glared straight into her eyes. She could see nothing, but she knew she was in deadly danger and instinctively put her foot hard on the brake. But there was no time to reverse, no time to do anything except to sit there at the mercy of the approaching monster. There was a terrible, sickening crash of metal against metal. The smaller car was tossed like a leaf over the low parapet, somersaulting as it went. It hit the bank and the crumpled remains slid backwards into the dark water of the River Tarl.

CHAPTER TWELVE

THERE was total darkness and a terrible pain in Fiona's chest which made every breath an agony. Slowly and painfully she returned to consciousness and became aware of confused noises and a splashing sound. Instinctively she tried to move, and found it impossible to shift even one finger. All the lower part of her body, she realised vaguely, was icy cold, which suggested it might be wet. Although she could see nothing at all, she seemed to know there was crumpled metal around, but she could remember nothing about the accident which had wrecked her car and done an unknown amount of damage to herself.

The pain in her chest was making it increasingly hard to breathe, though the air was fresh enough in spite of the strange, muddy smell. She moaned softly and tried to speak, but no words came.

A man's voice said quite near to her, 'She's conscious, Doctor.'

Doctor? What doctor? In her muddled mind she recalled that Max had something to do with accidents. Could it possibly be him?

'Fiona!' It *was* Max. There was no mistaking his voice, but she had never heard it sound so tender. 'We've sent for the firemen with cutting gear,' he went on, speaking slowly and clearly to make sure she could understand. 'They'll soon get you out of there. You've nothing to worry about—your head is well clear of the water. I'm afraid I can't get to you, love, but I'm right here beside you.'

Fiona wanted to tell him she was in pain, but it hurt even more to try and talk. Anyway, the last remnants of her brain reminded her, he wouldn't be able to give her the shot of morphine she so badly needed, because he couldn't reach her. Closing her eyes, she drifted away again.

The blare of a siren roused her and there were new noises, men shouting to each other, and metallic sounds as their powerful gear sliced through her poor little car as though it had been butter. Soon there was a blaze of light all around, so bright that she had to close her eyes again. The pressure on her chest eased, but the pain increased and she wanted to scream but again could only produce a low moan.

And there was Max, close enough to touch her gently. He said urgently, 'Try to tell me where it hurts most.'

Fiona made a great effort. 'My—my chest——'

'Your ribs too?'

'Yes.' Her head was cradled against his shoulder and she wanted it to stay there, but he laid her down gently on something soft and warm and got busy with a hypodermic. Surprisingly, in the midst of all the other pain, she felt a slight prick and once more slipped into a semi-conscious state.

She knew little of the ride in the ambulance except that Max was still with her, holding her hand in a firm grip and giving her comfort by the mere contact. Vaguely she was aware that he wore his yellow tabard with 'DOCTOR' across it, and she realised he must have been summoned to attend the accident.

The irony of it struck her suddenly. Last time they had been at the scene of an accident they had been on the same side, working together. Idiotically she tried to laugh, and made such an odd sound that he looked at her in alarm. He must have caught a glint of the amusement in her eyes, for he smiled too and squeezed her hand.

After that she knew nothing at all until she came round to find herself propped up in a high hospital bed, alone in a small, unfamiliar room. There was a cradle over her legs and a kidney dish on the locker beside her. They must be expecting her to feel sick, she reasoned, but she had no nausea, only a truly terrible headache. Her eyes wandered to the door, which was wedged open, and at that moment a middle-aged staff nurse came into view.

'Hello! So you're awake, then?' She came up to the bed and put her fingers on Fiona's wrist.

It still hurt to breathe, but it was nothing like the agony she had experienced earlier. She said, 'Max?' in a small, faint voice, and the nurse bent her head towards her.

'Doctor—Doctor——' Absurdly, Fiona couldn't remember his surname.

'Don't worry your head about him now, dear. I don't expect your memory has quite come back yet, but it'll be easier to remember in the morning.'

'When—will—it—be—morning?' Fiona managed.

'Goodness, not yet, I hope! It's the middle of the night and the best thing you can do is go to sleep. You've had an anaesthetic, you know, so it shouldn't be any problem. You're not in pain, are you?'

'Only—kind—of sore.'

'Yes, well, that's only to be expected after an accident like you seem to have had.' The nurse picked up a new-looking chart and made some entries on it.

'My—legs?'

'No fractures, dear, except a couple of small bones in your right foot, but your legs are very bruised and lacerated, which is why you've got a cradle over them. You also bruised the sternum and broke a number of ribs, but you're all bandaged up now, so you should be feeling more comfortable in a few days. Only do try not to breathe too deeply for a while.' She replaced the chart and turned to go, but paused at the door. 'Have you got a headache?'

'Terrible!'

'That's not to be wondered at. You've got concussion, you know, so that's another reason for keeping very quiet. Go to sleep now, like a good girl, and then the morning'll come more quickly.'

She was talking to her as though she'd been a wakeful child wanting it to be Christmas Day, Fiona thought crossly, and then remembered she had often done the same thing herself in her hospital days.

Obediently she closed her eyes, and the next thing she knew was a cup of tea being dumped on the locker, placed there by a weary-looking nurse with two stripes on her cap.

'Hello!' the girl said cheerfully. 'How are you this morning?'

'It really is morning now?'

'Oh, yes, we're in the thick of it. I let you sleep as long as I dared, but I'm afraid I'll have to wash you in a few minutes and make you look nice for the day. It looks as if you're going to get some visitors—the phone's been ringing already.'

'Who rang up?' Fiona asked eagerly, glad to find that speech wasn't so difficult this morning.

'How would I know? Staff answered it, but she did say your mother'd be along later on with some of your own nighties and other things——'

'My mother? Don't you mean my stepmother?'

The nurse shrugged. 'She's Mrs Shelton, anyway.'

To Fiona's thirsty mouth, the tea was like nectar. She submitted to being washed, but winced when the nurse attempted to brush her hair. When her breakfast came she managed to swallow some scrambled egg, but was obliged to leave the toast, since eating was even more painful than breathing. Her oesophagus must be bruised, just like most of the rest of her body. How long would she have to remain in hospital? she wondered.

She put the question to the young houseman who came to see her later on. He was thin and sandy-haired and looked as though he had been up all night, but he had retained a veneer of cheerfulness.

'You're a lot better this morning,' he told her, studying the chart. 'Any pain?'

There was no point in telling him she hurt more or less all over, with some parts worse than others. None of it was real pain, so she just said, 'My ribs, mostly. When can I be discharged?'

'I'll write you up some painkillers. Ask for them if you feel the need.' He scribbled busily. 'As for how long you'll have to stay here, that depends on whether there's anyone to look after you at home, but certainly you can't leave until the concussion wears off. Do your parents live locally?'

It was simplest just to say, 'Yes,' and that was what Fiona did, though she was not at all sure she wanted to go to Cornerways. For one thing, it didn't seem fair to Barbara.

At the door, the doctor paused with his hand on the knob. 'By the way, you must keep absolutely quiet for three days, and that means no visitors except parents. Definitely no boyfriends!' He grinned and disappeared.

Left alone, Fiona took herself severely to task. It was absurd to have hoped Max might come to see her. She had a very hazy memory of last night, but she thought he had been quite exceptionally nice to her.

Well, he would be, wouldn't he? She was a patient now and entitled to his tenderness and compassion. It was ridiculous to imagine there was any other reason for it. Besides, there was still Maggie.

Fiona sighed and experienced a wave of depression as she made up her mind to the certainty that she wouldn't get a visit from Max. No doubt he had rung up—since she was employed at the practice he would feel it his duty—but it wouldn't even occur to him to come and see her.

And even if he did come, what would be the point?

During the next few days she did as she was told, and rested quietly, just letting the world drift past her hospital room. She had expected to be moved to the main ward, but Sister let her remain in isolation— perhaps because she was a nurse and therefore privileged—and this helped her to live the life of a cabbage.

Her father and Barbara came every day, bringing

flowers, grapes, Lucozade and even chocolates. It was wonderful to see them, to feel she had a family again after years of doing without.

'Give us a ring when they say you can come home,' Colin said, 'and we'll come straight over to fetch you. You'll stay with us, of course.'

'I shall enjoy spoiling you,' Barbara assured her when she protested.

The three days were up on Sunday, but the surgeon who had dealt with her injuries ordered another two days' rest.

'You were very lucky not to get a punctured lung,' he said severely, looking at her over his half-glasses.

Fiona accepted the ultimatum without argument. She didn't feel in the least energetic, and although the headache had gone she had discovered a lump hidden in her hair which was extremely painful. Her memory had returned, and sometimes she wished it hadn't as her imagination painted over and over a picture of that huge car coming straight for her with its blinding lights. The driver had escaped with minor injuries, she'd been told, but he would have to suffer later on when the police brought a case against him.

On Sunday afternoon she was lazing in an armchair by the window, an unopened magazine on her lap, when there was a tap on the door. Perhaps it was Liz? She had sent a message to say she would come as soon as the restriction was lifted. Pleased at the prospect of a visitor, Fiona called, 'Come in!' and sat up expectantly.

But it wasn't Liz.

The door opened, letting in a babel of sound from

the ward, which was full of Sunday visitors, and suddenly Fiona's heart started beating at such a rate that her breathing was nearly as painful as on the day after the accident.

'I had to come and see for myself how you were.' Max entered with as much assurance as if he had been one of the resident doctors. He dumped a huge bunch of carnations on the bed table and advanced to stand in front of her. 'Good God—you look as fragile as a kitten! How are you feeling?'

'Fine!' She forgot the lingering aches and pains and gave him a brilliant smile.

'Why are you still here, then?' He glared at her accusingly, his blue eyes very bright, as though he thought she might be malingering.

Fiona shrugged and grimaced as her ribs protested. 'Doctor's orders. I'm only the patient.'

'They say it's good for us to see the other side of the coin,' he remarked, sitting on the edge of the bed. 'Can't see why myself.'

'I can. I've learnt a lot while I've been here.'

'Huh!'

He had not taken his eyes from her face since he came into the room, and Fiona found her own held by the steady gaze. After the few commonplace remarks they had made to each other the air was suddenly so full of tension she could hardly bear it.

Max stood up again abruptly and reached her in one long stride. He said in a strangled voice, 'Oh, Fiona darling—I'm afraid to touch you!' and dropped to his knees, reaching out to slide his arms round her neck and draw her closer.

Her lips trembled as she waited for his kiss in a state

of delirious disbelief, but instead of taking possession
of her mouth in his usual masterful way, he pressed his
cheek against hers with a sort of desperation and went
on talking. And what he said was so incredible that she
scarcely dared to believe she had heard right.

'I've tried hard, but it's no good—I can't hide it from
you any longer. When I knew you were trapped in that
crumpled car I nearly went out of my mind. I knew
then that I'd just got to tell you——'

Somehow Fiona found her voice. As Max broke off
to struggle with emotion, she lifted her hand and
smoothed back the unruly hair on his bowed head.
'Please—don't make me wait. I don't think I can bear
it. What do you want to tell me?'

He raised his head then and looked straight into her
eyes. 'I love you, Fiona. My heart and soul and body
are all yours, whether you want them or not. I want to
love and cherish you for the rest of my life, but——'
He broke off again and then finished with a rush, 'Is
that what *you* want? Because if it isn't——'

'Oh, Max, I love you too!' She leaned forward and
kissed him tenderly on the mouth, and then suddenly
passion leapt between them and she pressed both hands
against the back of his head to make the contact closer,
and closer still.

Neither of them noticed another tap on the door, but
some sixth sense caused Fiona to look that way. The
door was opening and she knew she had another visitor.
She made a small, strangled sound and Max, fearing
that he had hurt her, released his grip. Seeing the
dismay in her eyes, he turned his head to discover the
cause of it.

Maggie McBride stood transfixed in the doorway,

one hand clutching the lintel and the other holding a big bouquet of sweet peas. She was staring, her mouth slightly open and a ridiculous expression of astonishment on her face.

For a moment there was total silence. It was as though they had all three been frozen into a tableau. Then Max rose to his feet in a leisurely way and said in a carelessly friendly tone, 'Hi, Maggie!' as he moved to stand with his back to the window.

Fiona's brain worked frantically, but all she could find to say was, 'What lovely flowers! I adore sweet peas,' in a high, artificial sort of voice.

'You don't really need them, do you?' Maggie still stood in the doorway, her face unnaturally pale. 'I see you've already got some carnations, so I'll dump them in the ward and then disappear, since it's obvious I came in at the wrong moment.' There was intense bitterness in her voice, but she managed to add in a more normal manner, 'It's great you're so much better, Fiona.'

After the door had closed behind her, Max said furiously, 'God! I wouldn't have had that happen for the world.'

'I don't suppose you would.' Fiona surprised herself by the calmness of her comment. The dream had been wonderful while it lasted, but it had ended pitifully soon. 'Don't you think you'd better leave too? You might be able to catch Maggie up and——'

He ran his hands through his hair. 'What the hell makes you think I'd want to do that?'

'Surely it's obvious? You must admit you owe her an explanation——'

'I'll admit nothing of the sort!' Max shouted.

Fiona leant her head back against her pillows as exhaustion overwhelmed her. The high level of emotion which she had been experiencing during the last few moments would have taken it out of anyone and was certainly quite unsuitable for someone recovering from concussion.

Max noticed the movement and was instantly contrite. 'My poor darling, you shouldn't have been subjected to all this, but how was I to know Maggie would turn up?' He retreated to his original seat on the bed and regarded her anxiously. 'Could you bear to talk a little longer? There's a lot that needs sorting out.'

'You're right there.' Fiona struggled to regain her composure. If Max left now, she wouldn't be able to rest, that was for sure. Much better to get everything sorted out and then try to forget.

And yet—he had said he loved her. Surely he wouldn't have done that if it wasn't true? But, in that case, what about Maggie?

'The whole village believes you're going to marry Maggie,' she said bleakly.

He was horrified. 'It's even worse than I thought! Did you believe it too?'

'I didn't know what to think.'

'Hell—what a mess!' Max leapt up again and began to walk up and down the room. 'I'll tell you the whole story and all you've got to do is lie still and listen, so just relax and leave it to me.'

Relax! Fiona's lips twitched wryly, but she closed her eyes and contrived to give the impression of obeying the instructions.

'Maggie and I have always been friends. We trained together, you know, so it's a long-standing friendship.

But I swear it was nothing more until the night of her father's stroke. I brought her back from the hospital and she was in a bit of a state. Foolishly, I gave her a stiff whisky and it went to her head. She—she begged me to stay—said she couldn't bear to be alone. Well, of course, I couldn't possibly agree to that even if it only meant remaining in the house, but she was really quite distraught and I had to help her undress, which was most embarrassing.'

He paused, frowning, but Fiona gave no sign of wishing to comment, and he continued.

'The result of all this was that I said I'd stay until she went to sleep. I was hoping, of course, that the whisky would send her off quite quickly, but actually it was some time before I dared to leave.' He paused by Fiona's chair. 'I suppose somebody saw me?'

'Yes. Anne's Auntie Dot.'

'There's not much she misses, but until now I'd always thought it was rather a joke.' He gave a short, humourless laugh. 'I guessed there was talk going on, but I didn't let it bother me. My chief worry was Maggie herself. I couldn't possibly be sure how much she remembered, but I had a nasty suspicion she believed our relations had—er—advanced somewhat.' Resuming his former position on his knees, he gazed anxiously into Fiona's face, his eyes begging for understanding. 'I was in a hell of a fix because I didn't feel I could drag it out into the open while Maggie was so worried about her father.'

'I can understand that, but why did you let it go on so long?' Gathering all her strength, Fiona prepared to do battle for her happiness. If they didn't get this sorted out now so it could be tidied away and—eventually—

forgotten, it would lie between them forever, constantly liable to spring to life in moments of stress.

'You said a little while ago,' she went on carefully, 'that you loved *me*. Do you think it was kind to treat me the way you did so that I was all confused and hung up and couldn't understand what was happening?' Max was silent so long that she began to feel frightened. 'Why don't you say something?' Her voice rose in agitation. 'Is it because you *can't* explain it?'

He had been frowning down at his folded hands, which rested on her lap, but now he looked up and faced her honestly. 'One reason was that I was a coward. I kept putting off extricating myself from the situation I'd got into. I couldn't think how to tell Maggie she'd got it all wrong. Besides, nothing had actually been *said*. I might have been the one who was wrong.'

Fiona nodded sympathetically. 'I can appreciate that, and I know men absolutely hate anything uncomfortable of that sort.'

He pressed a kiss into the palm of her hand. 'Bless you for saying that, darling.'

'Did you have another reason?' she asked. 'You rather gave me that impression.'

'The other reason is considerably less shame-making. I was very far from being certain how you felt about me. In fact, you made it quite plain on more than one occasion that you didn't even like me. It just didn't occur to me that I was making you suffer. I thought it quite likely that the past was still more important to you than the present. You were terribly tangled up in memories when you first came to Tarling and I had no real reason for thinking you'd changed.'

'I struggled free of that web of memory a long time ago,' Fiona told him. 'The present suddenly began to seem so much more important, but I didn't dare to think about the future.'

Max stretched out his arms and folded them round her with the utmost tenderness and care. 'It's the immediate future I'm thinking about at this moment,' he said with a smile. 'At least I hope it's fairly immediate. The day when I can take your body in my arms without having to remember it's fragile—the day when I can really show you how much I love you.'

Fiona wanted it too, but even as her heart began thudding in anticipation, she spared a thought for Maggie. She was a sensible girl, she would give herself a good talking to and make up her mind to get over her disappointment as quickly as possible. And perhaps, in the course of time, she would find another man whom she could love.

'You'll have to move out of the McBrides' house,' she said suddenly. 'You can't possibly go on staying there.'

'It was never a good idea, and, in any case, it was only meant to be temporary. I've been waiting for a vacant room at that guest-house where Barbara stayed once. I'm moving in tomorrow, thank goodness.' He began kissing her lightly and yet sensually, his lips exploring her whole face, but as they reached her mouth he paused for a moment. 'Directly you're strong enough, my darling, we must start looking for our own house. You *did* say you'd marry me, didn't you?'

Fiona smiled. 'I don't think you asked me, but I will—of *course* I will!'

He kissed her rapturously. 'We must try and find a

house you can love as much as you used to love
Cornerways——'

'More than Cornerways,' she interrupted. 'Much,
much more!'

She didn't need to tell him the reason. It was shining
in her eyes and made plain by the tender curve of her
lips. Cornerways couldn't compete with a house shared
with Max, no matter how much they argued about
reflexology and probably other things as well. Their
home would be their haven, a place where they would
love each other, and bring up their children, and be
happy.

A ROMANTIC TREAT FOR YOU AND YOUR FRIENDS THIS CHRISTMAS

Four exciting new romances, first time in paperback, by some of your favourite authors – delightfully presented as a special gift for Christmas.

THE COLOUR OF DESIRE
Emma Darcy

CONSENTING ADULTS
Sandra Marton

INTIMATE DECEPTION
Kay Thorpe

DESERT HOSTAGE
Sara Wood

For only £5.80 treat yourself to four heartwarming stories.

Look out for the special pack from 12th October, 1990.

60th
BEST SELLING ROMANCE

THAI SILK – Anne Weale　　　　　　　　　**£1.45**

Anne Weale has been writing for Mills & Boon for 35
years. Her books are sold worldwide and translated
into 19 different languages.
As a special tribute to Anne's success, Thai Silk, her
60th Mills & Boon Romance, has been beautifully
presented as an anniversary edition.
An intriguing love story . . . Not to be missed!

12th October, 1990